Praise for *Anthropology:*

"Rhodes has devised a perfect format for skewering those fleeting, hallucinatory flights of perverse fantasy that all lovers, both male and female, are so desperately prone to entertaining despite themselves." —*LA Weekly*

"Rhodes boils down the stories of love between men and women to their comic, sad, and mad essentials: why we want each other and why we repel each other."
—Jonathan Ames, author of *I Love You More Than You Know*

"Dan Rhodes is the master of a new art form. In the blink of an eye he tells you everything. He's a brilliant writer who puts lightning in the spaces between words and, in one paragraph, creates a world." —Matthew Klam, author of *Sam the Cat*

"One hundred and one stories, all about girlfriends. They cheat, they die, they leave, frequently. . . . The funny stories are all the funnier for being brief; the sad ones all the sadder for being sparse. Every one a twenty-second gem."
—*Maxim* (UK)

D0871004

Praise for *The Little White Car:*

"Younger readers and chick-lit aficionados doubtless will be its most appreciative readers, but this old crock enjoyed it, too."   —Jonathan Yardley, *The Washington Post*

"Witty . . . he certainly belongs on a list of the most gifted new fiction writers."   —*The New York Times Book Review*

"All manner of zaniness."   —*Los Angeles Times*

"A frothy, muzzy, comic caper . . . As fun and fast as a little white Porsche."   —*Publishers Weekly*

"A smart send-up of chick lit in a frothy French mode . . . Rhodes's satire . . . is smooth and deadly fun."
                    —*San Francisco Chronicle*

Praise for *Timoleon Vieta Come Home:*

"Mr. Rhodes [writes] with an anomalous blend of humor, heartfelt emotion and old-fashioned storytelling verve. He has written a beguiling and resonant little novel."
—Michiko Kakutani, *The New York Times*

"Rhodes's effortless prose and quick wit make him a master of the quip and character sketch." —*Publishers Weekly*

"Rhodes demonstrates his ability to spin an engaging tale time and again." —*The New Yorker*

"[Rhodes's] brief vignettes on emotionally (and often physically) scarred characters are charged with honesty, biting irony and humor." —*Time Out New York*

"*Timoleon Vieta Come Home* is by turns hilarious and heartrending. Rhodes is that real, rare thing—a natural storyteller." —*The Sunday Times* (London)

"A whimsical, menacing exploration of thwarted love."
—Sam Lipsyte, *The New York Times*

Don't Tell Me
the Truth About Love

Also by Dan Rhodes

Anthropology
The Little White Car
Timoleon Vieta Come Home

Don't Tell Me the Truth About Love

stories by

Dan Rhodes

CANONGATE
Edinburgh · New York · Melbourne

Thanks to the staff of the Creative Writing department at the University of Glamorgan (particularly Sheenagh Pugh) the luthier Calvin Talbot, Richard "Waste Disposal" Marshall, the city of Sheffield, H. F. Ryan, my siblings and, of course, W. B. and V. C. Rhodes.

The music for "The Carolingian Period" was written by Terry Edwards.

This edition published in 2005 by Canongate Books Ltd., Edinburgh

First published in Great Britain in 2001 by Fourth Estate, a division of HarperCollins*Publisher*

Printed in the United States of America

FIRST AMERICAN EDITION

ISBN 1-84195-738-0

Canongate
841 Broadway
New York, NY 10003

06 07 08 09 10   10 9 8 7 6 5 4 3 2 1

Come, be a man. Drown thyself? Drown cats, and blind puppies.

Iago

Contents

1
The Carolingian Period 1

2
The Violoncello 13

3
Glass Eyes 57

4
Mademoiselle Arc-en-ciel 73

5
Landfill 101

6
The Painting 147

7
Beautiful Consuela 153

Don't Tell Me
the Truth About Love

The Carolingian Period

The Professor sat behind his desk, dwarfed by his vast red leather armchair. He shuffled into an agreeable position, raised his left fist to his mouth, cleared his throat, turned to the student sitting before him on a frail wooden seat, formed his lips into a geometrically faultless circle and began.

Oc - ta- go- nal, domed struc - tures are by no means ex - clu - si - vely Ca - ro-
ling- i - an, but they so ty- pi- fy at least the po- pu- lar per - cep- tion of the
pe- ri- od that one might for - give one- self were, just for a flee- ting moment, one to
re- ckon the e - ra's Ger - ma- nic an- te- ce- dents to be, in fact, i - mi- ta- tive.

For thirty years he had begun his tutorials with this sentence. Now he could see flaws in it. It was far too flippant and perhaps a little convoluted, but he was not going to change it. For decades its playful tone had appeared to put his students at their ease, and he knew how important that was.

He was the showpiece of the School of Architecture, the one who, as a much younger man, had designed some truly outstanding buildings. He had passed in late middle age into a semi-retirement of high-profile lecturing, occasional appearances on television or the radio, and the publishing of enthusiastically received studies of Western Christian Architecture. As he had grown older his duties had been scaled down, but he retained his professorship. His only remaining functions were to deliver a single lecture each year, sit prominently at graduation ceremonies, and engage in a thirty-minute individual tutorial with every final-year student. The subject of this tutorial was always 'Ecclesiastical Structures of the Carolingian Period'. It was an area for which he had never had any great enthusiasm, and he had only agreed to cover it as a favour for a colleague whose name he had long forgotten. Insidiously it had made itself a fixture, and to have changed it at this late stage would have involved the filling in of forms, so it remained in place.

Still, he received no complaints because the students were always glad to meet at last the man of whom they had heard so much and caught only the briefest of glimpses, at his annual lecture or as he made a rare appearance passing through the campus. In the holidays they would return to their families with tales of having met him, showing them battered editions of his books, to which he would often add his signature, to emphasise the significance of this tutorial. So they would sit in the uncomfortable old seat, listen to very little (preferring to savour the learned atmosphere of his study), learn nothing of the Carolingian Period and leave.

He looked directly at the student as if expecting a response to this rhetoric. With the pretty fingers of her right hand she was pulling her bottom lip out as far as it would stretch, folding it down over her chin to expose its shiny crimson underside, and letting it snap back into its original position, ready to start the journey again. His gaze broke this cycle, and she turned red, sucked her lips into her mouth and sat on her hands, hoping he had not asked her to speak. When he carried on, seemingly unperturbed, she relaxed but was careful not to play with her mouth any more.

She looked at him and tried to understand. But no, she could not make out a single word he was saying. She still listened, though. To her ears his soft, slow speech sang like a peculiar musical instrument, one she had never before heard. As she concentrated on the sounds he made she began to catch the tiniest fragments of tunes, strange and lovely tunes that gently skipped and danced and darted, and were entirely new to her. The fusion of his pitch and tone created something almost too wonderful.

...and there are T-shaped ba-si-li-cas at al-most ev'-ry turn.

He had delivered this tutorial so many times that he no longer had to think of the words as they left him. So as he spoke, his mind was apt to leap to any of an infinite number of destinations. This time it focused straight on to the beauty of the girl before him. She was wearing a tiny summer dress with flowers on it that left the pink, smooth plains of her shoulders, arms and crossed legs open to his view. Her brown eyes darted around the room, and whenever they met his she flashed a smile so sweet that his heart melted, and he forgave her for so clearly paying no attention to his tutorial.

She continued to wonder what the old man was talking about. He seemed so nice, and just as an old man should be.

He smelled of pipe tobacco and kept his window closed to the fresh summer air outside. That seemed right, somehow. As he carried on speaking she considered spending more time on her English. She had always learned enough to see her comfortably through exams, but as soon as the teacher told them to put down their pens, it all vanished. Now she was over from France for an exchange year, she realised everyone would expect her to know quite a lot of the language and she felt a little ashamed that she could not understand a word this dear old man was saying in his wonderful voice. She so wanted to talk to him about this and that. She looked at his tweed jacket and his messy white hair, and wished he was her great uncle, and she his favourite grandniece of four who was allowed to clamber upon his knee.

Fortune ensured that she would never know her appointment with him had been a clerical error and that in the room directly above, her personal tutor sat in his office staring at an empty chair and wondering where the French girl had got to. He looked at the photograph that was clipped to her details, and sighed. She was so, so pretty.

And of course The Professor thought so too, but she was not the only girl this pretty he had known. In fact he had met many young women as lovely as her when he had been a handsome, fairly wealthy young man who stood erect over six feet tall, had a head of thick, dark brown hair and had often made appearances in the national press. He had even been a regular in the Eligible Bachelor columns of society magazines. Consequently he had been introduced to a stream of charming and beautiful heiresses, actresses, debutantes and dancers. After a courteous chat with these ladies he would drift away, leaving them alone and melancholy and prime targets for the ever-circling pride of unmarried men that stalked these affairs. He had always felt uneasy at such social occasions, but they were a part of his job. He had to meet the most influential people in order to win commissions, and it was a game he was compelled to play. Even so, he was always saddened by the sight of a handsome woman whom he had rejected leaving a party on the arm of another. But he knew that he could devote himself to one thing only, and that to take on a wife would be to do both of them a disservice. He had to pursue his architectural vision, and only when he had realised it could he think about finding and marrying a sweet and lovely girl.

As his mind drifted back to those days, he found that all the women he recalled had been replaced in his memory by the girl who was sitting before him and unwittingly weaving plaits from the thick black hair, a precious gift from her Tonkinese Montagnard grandmother, that tumbled down to her waist.

Wal - king in - to the Pa - la - tine cha - pel of Charle- magne at Aa - chen one

feels al - most as if one is in the mau - so - le - um of The - o - do - ric.

At this, the girl came to life and clapped her hands excitedly in front of her face, her half-plaited hair hanging in wild, abandoned bunches. At last she had understood some of the wonderful sounds coming from the old man's mouth. She had been to this chapel two summers previously with her sister and her aunt. She smiled at the memories of that holiday, and loved the old man a little more for making her so happy.

The clapping girl began to destroy his heart, piece by piece. All he wanted was to be young again, to be that sought-after young man. Then he could have taken her away to a life of adventure and romance. He really could have done it, too. He could have had a wife every bit as pretty and as sweet-natured as she clearly was, a wife he would have loved, and loved so totally that he would never have needed the pointless dreams he had clung to for so long.

He had been blinded by visions of cathedrals, palaces and entire cities, waiting to be built. His plans for them had been so exhaustive that he prepared not only for them to become thriving epicentres of commerce and politics, but also for the inevitable societal implosion to follow, when order and vitality drained from their civilisations and his structures stood neglected and abused. Then they were to begin their second lives, as ruins to endure for millennia. His journeys to Athens, Rome and Angkor had shown him the beauty of such ruins, and it was with rogue creepers, looters, vandals and the merciless elements in the forefront of his mind, that he approached his drawing board. For years on end he had locked himself away, believing that one day these awesome structures would become reality.

After the war he had been acclaimed for his contributions to the reconstruction of blitzed cities. Yes, he had designed fine town halls, museums and galleries, but those were hard times and he had found himself hampered by councils and committees, policies and budgets. There was always something there to stop him from coming even close to fulfilling his visions. His work was highly esteemed and he picked up a stream of plaudits and awards, but this meant little to him for he knew his best work had not been seen. As he grew older he slowly became resigned to the sober truth that the buildings in his mind would never be lived or worked in, would never be visited by streams of people from all over the globe, and would never decay into magnificence. As his confidence faded he tried to immerse himself in day-to-day work, to forget all his hopes and think of only the realistic, the attainable. It was no use. The visions remained, entire vistas of his own creation, but they had come to mock him like monstrous nightmares.

He wished he had been an artist. Then he could simply have assembled brushes, paint and canvas, and the images in his mind would be there for all to see. Or a writer, who requires no more than a pencil and a sheet of paper to capture his thoughts. To realise his ideas the architect needs so much more, more than he could ever hope to attain. He needs the means to create entire civilisations.

As he looked at his student, he beheld another vision. Even at his age he still longed to create, but now he knew it would never happen, that it was all just whimsy. He saw a walled city built in the shape of this perfect girl. Only from the air could you see the beauty of its contours, and . . . No, there was no point in even thinking about it. No point at all.

The tutorial came to a close without either of them really noticing. There was a silence during which The Professor and the girl looked at each other. Eventually they realised he had finished, and she stood up to leave. She could not go without saying goodbye to the old man so she walked towards him, to behind his desk where she held his hands, softly kissed his cheek and tried a little English.

Thank you. You are a ve - ry love- ly, ve - ry nice old man. Good - bye.

Her voice was the sweetest music he had ever heard. As she placed a final kiss on his other cheek he gently squeezed her hands and felt the weight of a lifetime of wasted opportunity crash down upon him.

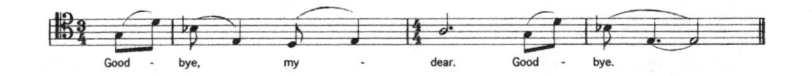

Good - bye, my - dear. Good - bye.

With one last smile she dashed out of the room, and The Professor tried to pull his thoughts into order. He looked through the closed window and down at the diamonds of grass and the students milling around in the sunshine. There was a knock at the door, and after a long pause it opened without him answering.

A very serious-looking young man approached, nervously nodded a greeting and sat in the still-warm wooden seat. Still looking out of the closed window, The Professor shuffled into an agreeable position, raised his left fist to his mouth and cleared his throat. He saw the girl run across the grass towards a young man who had been waiting for her. He was handsome, stood erect over six feet tall and had a head of thick, dark brown hair. In agony The Professor looked on. The handsome young man opened his arms and the girl fell into them, looking in wonder upon her lover's face. The Professor formed his lips into a geometrically faultless circle, and saw their bodies fuse in a delirious kiss.

The serious student of Architecture had heard tales of The Professor's extended pauses, and did not like to say a word. He sat patiently for five, ten, fifteen minutes. Finally, after twenty-five minutes, at the precise moment the beautiful couple made their love real on the floor of the young man's room, The Professor's old body slumped forward and the serious student of Architecture ran down to the reception to call for an ambulance.

The Violoncello

I

Ngoc lived with her mother, father and five younger brothers a long way down one of the alleys off Duong Dien Bien Phu. From the back of their small house you could look through the trees and over the dirty lake to the lights of Cong Vien Van Thanh, a fortified pleasure-park that tried its hardest to be Disneyesque. There, lovers would meet to share expensive soft drinks and illicit bursts of pleasure in any gloomy corner they could find. Ngoc had been there a few times, and it always made her smile to see the swan-shaped pedal boats innocently bobbing in the distant phosphorescent glow, because she knew exactly what was happening in them. For most it was more or less the only way they could be alone together, out of reach of prying eyes and ears. Despite their hard little benches and pedals that could shave the skin off your shins if your foot slipped off for a fraction of a second, they were an oasis away from the home and family.

Ngoc felt an affinity with the two-strong crews of these distant swans, because she had to get away too. Away from the dubbed voices of Hong Kong kung fu videos shouting from the open windows of every other house. Away from the Karaoke machine the family next door hardly ever stopped using. Away from her brothers who spent every minute they weren't watching their favourite fighting videos re-enacting them at high volume all over the house, squawking at each other in emulation of the Cholon accents of the dubbed voices.

So every Sunday, Tuesday and Friday evening at seven she would carry her 'cello in its case away from this noise, and along to where the alley widened and a xich lo waited. There was never any need for her to speak to the driver because for the past two of her nineteen years she had, except when the rain had been just too heavy and hardly anyone left their houses, made the same long journey at the same time on the same three days of the week.

On this evening she put the case on the floor where her feet should have gone, hopped up into the little bit left of the seat and crossed her legs. The driver pedalled the usual route into central Saigon, and all the way Ngoc was absorbed in her dreams of the music she would be playing when she got there.

The 'cello had been in the house for as long as she could remember. No one could explain how it had got there. When she was small her father had told her that it had been left behind by the French, but nothing more. How it had come to be lurking unloved and unused in a corner of their living room was a mystery to her. Whatever its history, it was old and looked very weary. Its body was covered in scratches and gashes, which was probably just as well because if it had been a beauty it would have been sold long before she had ever thought to take it from its case and try to play it.

The xich lo driver pulled up in the bay in front of the steps of the Library of Social Sciences on Ly Tu Trong, and Ngoc jumped out. She wrestled the 'cello down on to the pavement and paid the driver, who disappeared into the river of evening traffic.

Ngoc had started to play when she was fifteen. She would sit in the house, trying to ignore the background noise as she self-consciously scraped vague tunes to the protestations of her family and the crying of her youngest brother, who was then not even two. So she had looked for other places to play, where she would neither be bothered nor bother others. She visited quiet corners of parks, but these were dangerous in the evenings so she could only go on Sundays and in the school holidays, while it was still light. Even then, a heroin addict with empty black eyes and dirty matted hair had tried to steal the 'cello. She had wrested it back like a mother saving her child from a cradle-snatcher, and in the battle had picked up a deep gash above her eye. This marked the end of her time in parks. She began to play outside small cafés in quiet streets, away from which she was gently eased by kind but exasperated proprietors. She had even tried the solitude of a pedal swan, but it was expensive and a difficult shape, and anyway her every mistake flew across the still water and into the critical ears of the lovers under the trees on the shore.

The steps of the library had unexpectedly proved to be the most successful location. At first Ngoc had thought it was a stupid place to play and felt a little embarrassed being there, but once she had settled in she never found a reason to try anywhere else. In the evening the building was closed and empty, so there was no one inside to hear her and send her away. Ly Tu Trong was a busy street, but most of the traffic at this time of day was so thick that people couldn't take their eyes from the road ahead, and the few pedestrians who passed were so fixed on their destinations that they paid her little attention.

Often a pair of girls around eight and ten years old, probably sisters, would sit with her and listen to her play while counting the money they had collected selling gum on Dong Khoi. Some nights they would giggle and play, and others, when they hadn't sold much, they would crouch in silence and watch the traffic. Ngoc was always glad to see them and gave a smile whenever they arrived. If they looked sad, she would play a happy tune to cheer them up. She didn't know if it worked, but she hoped it did. In the two years she had been playing on the library steps they had been the only people who had heard her progress from making out-of-tune, almost random scrapings to beautiful music. She had never taken a lesson or even spoken to another 'cellist, and the layout of the three cramped steps, with their concrete bicycle ramp in the middle, forced her into an unusual, slightly awkward-looking position. Even so, she played and composed like a dream.

When her bow touched the strings, the roar of the tidal wave of Hondas faded away and she heard only the sounds she made with her battered old 'cello. As the piece ended the noise would return, but to Ngoc's ears it was the applause of a great concert hall. She always played for exactly one hour before heading home.

This Sunday evening the girls had not appeared and she packed up her 'cello alone. As she did, she saw a boy of about her age pushing his motorbike along the kerb. She had noticed him ride by quite often. He was very beautiful, but always a little over-made-up. He was looking for someone to mend his flat back tyre. He must have fallen off because there was a streak of dirt running down his long silver skirt and his red lips were sticking out in an angry pout. As he walked some of the people riding past slowed down and looked at him, smiling to themselves and their friends. One of three nasty-looking drunk boys on an ancient Super Cub 50 reached out and pulled his hair to see if he could score a wig. The shiny black mane was real, and Ngoc could see him holding back a tear as he rubbed the pain away. She wanted to sit him down beside her, play him a tune and make everything better, but she didn't know how to approach him.

As always, the same xich lo driver who dropped her off had failed to find any business elsewhere. Not that he ever tried too hard, preferring to sit and smoke with the other drivers. Knowing he had a return journey waiting, he was lurking around near the steps waiting for her.

As they trundled home they passed that boy. His bike was on its side, with the rear inner tube immersed in a bowl of water. For an instant his eye caught hers, and she smiled. So used to smirks and sideways glances, he turned away.

II

It was Tuesday evening, and Tuan needed somewhere quiet to study so he left his house, climbed on his Honda Dream II and drove over to the Library of Social Sciences. He hadn't been there before, but he thought he could vaguely remember hearing someone mention that it was open late and a pleasant place to study. He had begun to feel stifled at home and the idea of a total change of surroundings appealed to him. By the time he had put his bike in the giu xe and walked along Ly Tu Trong to the old French building it was nearly eight o'clock and the doors were long since closed. He paid no attention to the 'cellist playing on the steps, and she didn't notice him. He walked towards the door to see if there was a sign to tell him the opening hours, which there was. As he was reading it he could feel a presence by his side. Looking down he saw a little girl thrusting a packet of Wrigley's towards him. He ignored her but she wouldn't go away, so he lifted his right hand and waved it dismissively by his face. Without a word she sat back down next to her sister on the steps and listened to Ngoc's music.

Tuan's eyes followed her, and as they did he noticed the 'cellist, her face hidden by her long hair. He didn't know the tune she was playing, but liked it and crouched by the steps to listen. He didn't know it because Ngoc had written it in

19

the xich lo on her way over. After five minutes she finished, and Tuan pulled out five thousand dong. He threw it into the open case and walked away. He heard a voice behind him.

'Hey, you,' it said. He turned. 'No.'

The girl was pointing her bow at the note. If people gave her money the police might think she was begging, and arrest her or move her along. He walked back and picked it up. The sisters looked expectant. He gave it to the elder one, who smiled as he took a packet of gum from her basket. As he turned to go, Ngoc started to play again. More wonderful music. Walking away he glanced over his shoulder and saw her face for the first time.

Ngoc didn't know she was beautiful because no one had ever told her, but Tuan found himself looking at perfection. She was wearing cheap jeans with seams running down the front, and her brother's tatty Euro 96 T-shirt, but as he looked and listened he began to hover. He was too startled to stop moving and glided straight back to the giu xe for his bike, but for the next twenty-four hours he couldn't get her out of his mind. He went back the following evening to see if she would be there again.

She wasn't, and he became convinced that his life was ending. He sat in his spotless white shirt, his hair carefully sculpted, and waited. She didn't come. By half past nine he was certain that she had died in a terrible accident and he would never see her again. He went home feeling hollow.

The next day, Thursday, he did the same. He had given up smoking for nearly six months but that day, as he worried himself to distraction on the steps of the Library of Social Sciences, he started again. By Friday he was beginning to think that he had imagined her, and was almost at his wits' end. He took the day off university and sat in the library from the moment it opened, listening for signs and prepared at any moment for the last embers of hope to finally die. He was waiting to enter a state of mourning. He sat at a desk with some books open in front of him, but even though his eyes looked at the words, all he could see was her beautiful face concentrating on her playing, and all he could hear were the wonderful sounds she had made. He sometimes went out on to the balcony on the pretext of getting some fresh air, and looked down to see if she had arrived. Of course she never had. While the library was closed at lunch time he sat alone on the steps. Just after four-thirty he was prised from his seat by a librarian. He crouched outside, dejected and chain-smoking as the staff filed past him on their way home.

He wondered whether he should stay there for the rest of his life and imagine that the 'cello girl was beside him, playing her music and pausing between pieces to gaze longingly and adoringly at him. He might have to go and change his clothes and things occasionally, but he could remain on the steps more or less forever, immersed in the dream. After all, daydreams since the evening he had first seen the 'cellist were better than anything real he had ever known. If he thought hard enough it would almost be as though she were really there playing for him, and not lying dead at all. He remembered her skin. He had never seen anyone with perfect skin before. Not really perfect skin.

After fourteen cigarettes he finally made up his mind to abandon everything to wallow in his memories, and began to picture her in the spot where she had been sitting with her 'cello. The xich lo pulled up, and she got out. Emerging from the haze of his perfect delusion he didn't know whether to trust his senses, and sat frozen. She gave him a momentary smile of recognition and unpacked the 'cello. She was even more beautiful than he had remembered. She was growing her fringe out, and as she bent over her case a few strands landed in her eyes and she blew them away. Her bottom lip curled out.

Ngoc was happy to have an audience. Her confidence in her music was growing all the time, and she had always aimed to play in front of people one day, so she launched straight in. Tuan was transfixed. He listened and watched for the whole hour. Every note sent quakes through his heart, soul and the rest of his insides, and the sight of her in her tight bootleg Calvin Klein T-shirt almost made him lose control. When the hour was over she packed her 'cello away and gave him another smile as she lugged it over to the xich lo. He couldn't even say goodbye. He was worried that if he opened his mouth he would be sick, or his voice would pipe out like a castrato. When she had disappeared, he lit a cigarette and gradually drifted some of the way back down to the ground.

As the weeks floated by, Tuan became used to Ngoc's routine and was there every Tuesday, Friday and Sunday before she arrived. The gum girls turned up more often than not, and to Ngoc's delight the boy who had suffered the flat tyre would sometimes come and silently crouch on his big heels a short distance away from the others, his head tilted towards the 'cello as if the few extra centimetres would make a difference. A small, silent community was building up around her, and Tuan began to feel jealous. After three weeks he decided that the time had come to say something, if only au revoir. One Friday, as she was walking across the pavement to the xich lo with her case in her hand, after a quiet prayer he said, 'See you soon.' Ngoc smiled back at him, and replied.

'Yes. See you soon,' she said. The world stood still. The manic traffic on the street stopped dead. Even the noise froze into a uniform drone. When things snapped back to normality, she got into the xich lo and went home. He sat there with the girls and the strange boy for a full five minutes before they dispersed without a word.

Tuan felt sick, as though he had begun to live his whole life on that dangerous-looking fairground ride he had seen at the zoo but never dared to go on.

People started to notice the little crowd, and as Ngoc's playing got better and better her audience began to expand. They were joined by three small, dark brown boys with matted hair and holes in their oversized T-shirts. They would sit and listen together, dancing to the music if they could find a rhythm, and casting occasional glances at the gum girls to see if their antics had caught their attention. They rarely did. No one liked to step over the invisible boundaries that were starting to appear. Eye-contact, when it happened, was fleeting and awkward. They came alone or in their clusters, listened to Ngoc's 'cello, and then went away alone or in their clusters.

Whenever a foreigner was seen approaching on foot, the three boys would put one of their plans into action. At intervals of a few metres they would stagger into his path with their hands and arms twisted awkwardly, their eyes crossed and their tongues pressed hard into their bottom lips. Each would splutter the extent of his English: 'Hello Russian. Me from Campuchea.' Most foreigners automatically weaved their way through this human slalom, but sometimes the boys would make five or ten thousand dong, or even a dollar bill. This game was a constant source of amusement to them, and when they had made the money the whole façade would crumble; their eyes uncrossing as they rolled around helpless with laughter. The foreigner invariably walked on, feeling silly at having been duped. They never stopped to listen to the music.

Ngoc was oblivious to most of this. She appreciated her audience, but she was determined that they would not interrupt her playing at all. So for the full hour she played away, pausing only between pieces or to tune her instrument. Some pieces she had written before, some she made up as she played, and others she had heard here and there. At the end of the hour she would pack her case, smile back at everyone, nod in response to any au revoirs or thank yous or very goods, and go back to her family.

More regulars appeared. A policeman with two missing teeth came once to move Ngoc on. He stood waiting for her to notice him looming over her, but she carried on playing. By the time the piece ended and she came to, he was so captivated that instead of standing over her as she packed away and vanished, he simply said, 'That was beautiful. Thank you.'

'Not at all,' said Ngoc, and she began another tune. The policeman's wife had died the year before, and he had not been able to find happiness since. He took more bribes than ever, even more than when the baby was on the way, but they didn't make his days pass more quickly. After that evening, he would often stand a little way away from the group and listen.

Tuan was feeling more and more marginalised. He would watch Ngoc's strong, slender fingers dashing up and down the strings, and he knew that his were not the only pair of eyes watching them. His love for her was volcanic, and one evening he approached her.

'See you soon,' he said, as she clicked her case shut. She smiled and headed across the pavement to the xich lo. He followed. With everyone's eyes on him, he took the 'cello case from her and lifted it into the xich lo.

'Thank you,' said Ngoc, 'but there's no need.'

Shaking, Tuan whispered to her, 'Would you like to drink coffee?' She was surprised by this. Tuan looked at her face and felt crippled by her beauty. He had not seen her closely from this angle before, and he noticed a little nick in her right eyebrow where no hair grew. It was the only imperfection he could see, and of course he loved it as much as the rest of her.

She looked away. 'I have to get back to my family.'

She hopped into the xich lo and headed home. He glanced towards the people on the steps. They were all staring at him, and none of them were smiling. Their eyes followed him as he walked back to his motorbike.

When he was gone they went away.

One evening Tuan found that he was the only person there. Ngoc arrived, and he carried her case from the xich lo to the steps. 'There's really no need,' she said. As she unpacked he started a conversation.

'I think you play beautifully.'

'Oh no. Not really.' She spent a moment tuning up, then began a short piece. When it was over, he tried again.

'Would you like to drink coffee? My motorbike is just around the corner. We could go to Nguyen Hue.'

She was very gracious in her refusal. 'Thank you, but I have to play my 'cello. I have so little time.'

'But afterwards, before you go home?'

'No. I have to get back to my family.'

Tuan desperately searched for something to say. 'How many are there in your family?'

'Please,' said Ngoc, desperate to play again. 'I have to practise.' She launched into a sad, slow piece that she didn't even know was in D-minor, and the policeman appeared, standing a few metres away. Then the beautiful boy arrived to perch gracefully on the stone slab by the steps and cast the occasional uneasy glance towards the policeman. At the end of the evening Tuan didn't say goodbye. He sat there in his pressed clothes feeling small and stupid. He gave the dark boys a few thousand dong and went home.

*

Tuan's sisters had noticed him going out regularly, looking as though he were on his way to somewhere special. They began to tease him. 'Brother, what is her name? Is she beautiful? I think it's time you invited her home to meet your sisters.'

He felt awful whenever this happened. He couldn't say, 'This "she" is not what you think. You see I'm deeply in love with a girl who won't even speak to me beyond the call of courtesy. I, along with several others, sit close to her three nights a week for one hour at a time as she plays her violoncello, which she loves more than anything else; certainly more than she loves me.' It had been several months now, and despite her refusal to enter a friendship with him, his love for her grew. It made him feel uncomfortable, as helpless as a grain of rice being scorched in the sun and bullied by trucks and buses on the road to Vung Tau.

The crowd continued to grow, and with each new arrival he felt her drifting further away from his reach. He agonised over ways to make her notice him, to spend some time with him. For them to be together. But if she wouldn't even join him for a coffee on Nguyen Hue, his hopes for a lifetime of perfect love seemed laughable. He couldn't bear the way she tuned the battered old 'cello with her eyes closed and her head tilted, the way she smiled when she found the perfect pitch, the way she hammered, scraped or teased each note from it, the way she cradled it between her legs, and the gentle way she packed it away at the end of the evening. Sometimes he wanted to kick it into the traffic, to watch it splinter under the wheels of a passing truck. He still loved the music, though. He had never heard anyone play a 'cello the way she played hers.

That was because no one had ever played a 'cello like her before. By conservatoire standards she had taught herself badly, and had slipped irrevocably into terrible habits. But these habits worked, and she had become an extraordinary musician.

All he could do was sit and watch as she and the 'cello made their music together. He felt absolutely redundant, and in the depths of his unhappiness he began to make plans.

III

One Tuesday evening, Ngoc was slightly surprised to see that the smartly dressed boy was not waiting in his usual place when she arrived. She played for an hour to an audience of twelve, not counting the skinny baby sleeping in the arms of his blue-eyed mother. When she had finished she packed up, and everyone waited silently for her to disappear into the traffic before going back to their usual lives. Sitting in the xich lo, she thought only of her music and the scene she knew was awaiting her at home; her mother struggling to get her two youngest brothers off to sleep, and bellowing at them every time they sneaked out from under their mosquito net.

As they went over the junction with Hai Ba Trung she sensed a presence gliding along by her side. It was Tuan, wearing a very white shirt and sitting on his Honda Dream II.

'I'm sorry I missed you,' he said. 'I was busy.' He didn't tell her that he had been busy worrying about what he was going to say to her, and lying in wait along her route home.

'It doesn't matter.' Ngoc smiled.

'Are you doing anything at the weekend?'

'Yes, I am.' It was true. She always had something to do. When she wasn't helping her mother with the boys she was buried under a pile of textbooks. She was hoping to go to university to study English and Economics, and she used any free moments she found to try to capture the music in her mind, trying to hold it in place until she could find a chance to be with her 'cello. The music was always there, demanding to be played. This was why she so rarely missed a night on the steps.

'How about the next weekend?' Tuan asked.

'Yes, I'm busy then too.'

'We could go to Buu Long Mountain. You could take your violoncello.'

'I really can't spare the time.' And anyway, she didn't like Buu Long Mountain. She had been there eight times with her family and friends, and never wanted to go again. She would love to climb a real mountain and play her 'cello on the summit, but despite its name Buu Long Mountain barely even qualified as a hill, and was crawling with over-excited children falling into the brown waters of the old gravel pit masquerading as a magical hilltop lake. Sometimes they drowned and had their names read out on the television news. One day she would climb Mount Everest and play her 'cello at the top of the world, but the last place she wanted to go was Buu Long Mountain.

'It's very nice there,' yelled Tuan. 'Have you been?'

'Once or twice.'

'I would like you to come to my house and play for my family.' He was labouring in second gear, and shouting above the hum of his engine, the squeaking of the xich lo and the thunder of the rest of the traffic.

Ngoc had never even played to her own family since they had sent her elsewhere to practise. She would one day though, but only when she felt ready. She certainly wasn't about to play her music in a strange house, with its unfamiliar smells and alien cats rubbing against her legs.

'I'm sorry,' she shouted. 'I can't.'

'Well, when you can find some time please . . .' and as he was speaking a maroon Suzuki 250 driven by an American with a patchy beard clipped his back wheel and he flew off, landing in the middle of the road. The American, who looked drunk, somehow managed to keep his balance and sped away. Ngoc looked back to see if the boy was hurt. Traffic was swerving around him at high speed, missing him by inches. He was straight back on his feet, rubbing his leg and checking his bike for scratches.

The xich lo driver didn't stop laughing until the Daewoo sign on Xo Viet Nghe Tinh, and Ngoc tried as hard as she could but was unable to suppress a guilty smile.

Tuan had often laughed at rumours of a man in District Six who could do anything. Early the following Sunday he went to find him.

After a morning of asking around, he finally reached one of

a maze of streets glowing with red and golden incense sticks drying in the sun. He took a deep breath, and it was almost like being in a pagoda. He followed the directions he had been given, and found himself being led down the long corridor of a large house, and into a dark room with an unusually high ceiling. It smelled of noodles, and he couldn't make any sense of the Chinese writing all over the walls. He had tried to learn once, but had given up after two days. The man he had been seeking was sitting on the floor, finishing his meal. He wasn't quite as Tuan had expected; he was wearing a grey shirt and dark green trousers instead of vividly embroidered robes, and he didn't seem to exude any special aura. But at least he was quite old and had a long beard, even if it was a little disappointing in its wispiness and had what looked like a chunk of mushroom in it. Despite being born in Cholon the man had never spoken a single word of Vietnamese, and Tuan had even been told that he had never left his house. The fat, middle-aged woman who had opened the door introduced herself as his housekeeper and interpreted for him.

Tuan opened his mouth and his heart came out. He told of their first encounter, her music, her hair, her delicate ankles, the little bald spot on her eyebrow, everything. Initially he felt embarrassed speaking to a woman of his love for the 'cellist and his plans to be with her, but she did not snigger or even smile as he blurted out his story. Likewise, the man listened very carefully to the interpretation of what Tuan had to say, nodding his head and casting him the occasional glance.

In between mouthfuls of noodles, the old man made his reply to the housekeeper in a few short sentences. She translated: 'He says he can help you. But even though you have heard, as have so many others, that he can do any-thing, this is sadly not true. Do you have any money?'

'I have got two-hundred-and-forty American dollars,' Tuan replied. His grandfather had died the year before. The old man laughed without smiling, cleaned his beard with a paper napkin and went back to his bowl.

'And I have a Honda. If you can do what I ask, you can have that too. I will have no need for it. It's a Dream II. It's a year and a half old. It's never given me any trouble.' There was a short conference in Chinese.

'Then yes, he will do this for you.'

'But you said that he can't do everything. Can he do what I have asked? And how will I know that he will?' The old man seemed to understand this, and barked angrily at his housekeeper. Tuan was nervous. For the first time since entering the house he thought of his sisters. If he went through with this he would never see them again. He began to reconsider, but the image of the 'cellist was too strong to resist.

'He is a man of his word,' the housekeeper interpreted.

'But what is it that he cannot do?'

'He cannot make 'cellos.'

'Then what use is he to me?' cried Tuan.

'Listen to me,' snapped the housekeeper. 'He cannot, as you request, turn you into a 'cello. But, he can turn you into the raw material. The wood. The best wood in Vietnam.'

'But that's no good. If my girl is given a lump of wood she will hardly be inclined to take it home, cherish it, press her legs around it and run her pretty fingers up and down it for the rest of her life, will she? I am not going to leave my family and give up everything just to be picked up from the steps of the Library of Social Sciences by a passing scavenger and sold as firewood.'

'And,' the housekeeper continued as if he hadn't said a word, 'we know of a man who makes 'cellos. To the highest degree.' She looked directly at him, and he felt like a naughty child. 'Listen to me. Everyone who comes to us with a request like this always thinks they are the first, that their case is so unique, and that no one could ever understand what they are going through. Do you know how many people go missing each year in Ho Chi Minh City?'

'I don't know.' He looked at the floor and shuffled. 'A lot, though.'

'Yes, a lot. And do you know how many of them are missing because they have been turned into musical instruments to be handled and caressed by the people they love, but who they have come to accept will never love them back?'

'No. No I don't.'

'Well, we have done thirty-six in the last two years alone. Thirty-six. We are not amateurs, young man. Just last week we finished turning a civil servant into a guitar so he could be fingered and plucked by the man from his alley whom he had silently adored for twenty years without ever having dared to reveal his feelings.'

'And did it work?'

'I followed up on this two days ago and yes, the man was sitting on his true love's knee being played most attentively. I was unable to see the appeal of the guitarist in question, and the popular songs he was playing were hardly to my taste, but I believe our client to be very happy, if not elated at the situation. And he is just one of many.'

Tuan still had reservations. 'But if I become a pile of wood, what will happen to the shavings as the violoncello is crafted? Will my essence be swept into the fire? Will only a part of me live on? And what if that part cannot feel the touch of her fingers?'

When he heard this the old man erupted, and the house-keeper translated in her dry, flat voice: 'You foolish boy. Your essence will be bottled and kept safely here until the 'cello is ready and made to perfection. Only then will it be returned to inhabit the matter. Do you think he would trust a craftsman with your inner self?'

'No,' replied Tuan. He turned to the old man. 'I am very sorry if I have offended you.' This was interpreted and acknowledged with a stern nod.

'Shall we proceed now?' asked the housekeeper.

After receiving the old man's word that the 'cello would be of exemplary quality, and that it would be delivered to the girl as she played her old battered instrument on the steps of the Library of Social Sciences, he handed over his two-hundred-and-forty dollars and wheeled his motorbike into the house.

Within three hours he was a bundle of spruce, maple, ebony and sycamore being transported on a trolley to a workshop on Nguyen Thien Thuat, District Three.

IV

That same evening, Ngoc began to wonder why the boy who had asked her to Buu Long Mountain had not come to listen to her music. She didn't give this a great deal of thought, but she had become used to him being there and as she went home she half expected him to be waiting for her somewhere down the road. He wasn't. As weeks passed and he failed to reappear it became a little strange and unsettling that the space he had so regularly occupied on the steps, the one closest to her, was usually either empty or filled with somebody else. A Japanese student of the Vietnamese language sat there once or twice a week, always on her own. She had tried to start a conversation once, but Ngoc couldn't understand a word she was saying so she just smiled at her. Ngoc hoped that she hadn't hurt the boy's feelings by not joining him for coffee or going to Buu Long Mountain with him, and she felt a little sad. It reminded her of the time her neighbour's old dog had disappeared.

All this time, Tuan was being turned from a few blocks of wood into a meticulously crafted 'cello. For the whole of the transition his body lived in the District Three workshop, but his essence was in a green bottle in District Six, so the pain of the reconstruction was removed from him. Nevertheless, nearly every day he felt a step or two closer to his goal. As the gouge began to shape him, and the scrapers to fine him down, he could somehow sense it happening. There was an odd kind of communication between his essence and the matter. When the luthier had gone to visit his brother in Dac Lac Province for six days, Tuan sensed that no progress was being made, and felt uneasy. When work resumed he was very relieved. He was still frightened, but he had faith in his decision and longed for the day when he and the girl would become lovers.

During the many weeks he spent inside the bottle he sometimes thought of his family, particularly his sisters, and every time an overwhelming sadness came over him. He soon learned to combat this by picturing the girl. The way she would sometimes let the neck of her 'cello rest between her beautiful breasts. Her lips that she would press upon the scroll of the instrument as she pondered what to play. Her little wrists that looked as though they would snap at any moment as they sent the bow into the strangest angles. Her long, slender legs. Her long, slender fingers. The fingers that would never wear his ring, but would touch him with love until death came between them.

Ngoc's days floated by in the pattern she and several others had become used to, but everything was soon to change. She had finally gained a place at the university, and was due to start after the long vacation. She worried that her studies would keep her from her 'cello. Some classes were in the evening, and it seemed inevitable that her routine would be interrupted. Also, she worried that with home-study she might have no time for music at all. This frightened her. She thought about the possibility of finding the occasional quiet minute or two to practise at home as she had done when she first tried to play. Now that she was beginning to make more melodious sounds it might not be such a problem. It wasn't ideal, but if it was the only way she could carry on making her music it would have to do.

If she had to stop going to Ly Tu Trong she would miss the crowd on the steps, even though she had never really spoken to them. Theirs was an invisible bond, and it wouldn't be easy to break.

Most of the time she tried to forget about all this, and carried on as usual. She decided to wait until she received her timetable before getting really upset about it. Still, some evenings as she glanced over to the gum sisters or the policeman, she wondered what they would do without her. Where would they go at this time instead of the steps of the library? What would they do? She imagined the blue-eyed woman not rocking her baby, neither of them wearing calm expressions as they gently swayed to the music, but instead wandering along some street or other with a plastic bowl in her hand, asking strangers for a few hundred dong and impatient restaurateurs for dollops of food. She pictured the beautiful boy, not shyly tilting his head towards the 'cello and smoking a cigarette through the side of his scarlet mouth, but picking up men on The August Revolution Road. They would have nothing to look forward to. No break from their lives, just work. Or whatever it was you called what they did. At night she would sometimes feel a tear slip out, and as she wiped it away she realised how much they meant to her. If she felt a sense of loss after the disappearance of the slightly annoying boy, how could she ever leave them all?

Initially, progress had been very slow. The luthier worked meticulously, happy to have such high-quality materials and determined to make the finest 'cello of his career. Tuan's parts were distributed around the workshop; his front was on top of a cupboard, his neck on a shelf under the workbench. This made him feel incomplete, though he didn't know why. He was still apprehensive but his maker worked on him a little almost every day, despite having other instruments to attend to, and this reassured him.

The final stages were swift, and Tuan felt this from the confines of his bottle. The ribs were moulded with a hot bending iron, and this gave him a warm, satisfied feeling. When the parts finally came together and were glued firmly into place, he felt stronger and more confident than ever. Flawless soundholes were cut into his belly, and the luthier stood back to admire his work.

Tuan was coated with boiled linseed oil, then varnished. When the final coat had dried, he was finished with Tripoli powder and more linseed oil. Then he was strung and tuned, and ready to be played. Nervously, his maker picked up his bow and began. The sounds Tuan made were like nothing the luthier had ever heard. His tone was rich and resonant, and on hearing this music his wife came down from their apartment to listen. She heard the way the sounds filled the workshop, even though its acoustics usually squashed music flat. She knew her husband had never made such a 'cello before, and her heart filled with pride. They felt like school teachers waving a favourite pupil into the world when, the next day, they packed it into a case and took it over to the old man from District Six.

He was sleeping, and was not happy to be woken up. The 'cello was handed over. With a grunt he paid the outstanding money, and went back to sleep.

Tuan could only guess what had been going on all this time, but he felt unusually strong and ready to leap into his new life. He didn't know that his body was just feet away from him and it would only be a couple of hours before the transition was complete.

The old man finally woke up, wandered over to the shelf where Tuan lived alongside the bottled essences of eight others, and picked him up. Blearily he made his way over to the 'cello case and opened it. He hadn't even bothered to look at it when it was delivered, and despite his initial indifference he was impressed. It was the most handsome instrument he had ever commissioned. The grain was beautiful, the varnish deep, and the ebony fingerboard was perfect. There were no rough edges, no scratches, nothing. He nodded his approval to himself and carefully sprinkled Tuan's essence on to the instrument. He closed the case and called to his housekeeper for a bowl of rice.

Ngoc's twentieth birthday fell on a Sunday, and she enjoyed the celebrations. Her mother made a beautiful meal for the family which lasted well into the afternoon. One of her old school friends had made the journey from her home in Ben Tre Province, where she was living with her new husband, and his family. After the others had fallen asleep and were spread all over the floor with their mouths open, they talked for a long time about what they had been up to in the years since they had last met. Ngoc told her about the steps of the Library of Social Sciences and all the people who came to listen to her. Because it was her birthday she had planned to stay in with her brothers, but her friend begged her to go to the steps so she could see all these people first-hand. So they loaded up the xich lo, squashed themselves in and went.

*

As they reached their destination, Tuan was still in District Six, inside his case and being hauled up on to a motorbike to be sent across the city and presented to her. He had no idea that the timing was so perfect; a gift on her twentieth birthday. He was petrified. Initially he had felt good in his new body, and the lining of the case was furry and comfortable, but as he felt his journey to the steps commence, all his doubts suddenly surfaced. What if she was not there? What if she had moved away? What if the driver were to steal the 'cello and he ended up being played by someone else? He tried to quell these fears as he had done before, but he couldn't. For the first time he regretted ever having done this. He felt stupid. He had thrown everything away for nothing, and imagined his poor mother's despair at his disappearance. The realisation of the magnitude of his mistake plunged him into a state of hopeless confusion and he thought he should cry, but he couldn't.

That evening, Ngoc's friend sat in Tuan's old place on the steps and had the time of her life. All the people she had heard about turned up, and she smiled at them as if they were old friends. She bought some gum from the girls and handed it to the dirty boys, who swallowed it within seconds. She listened as Ngoc played perfectly, making the 'cello weep beautiful laments and sending songs of hope sparkling through the unrelenting ugliness of the traffic noise. She remembered Ngoc telling her that she might have to stop playing on the steps, and the looks of perfect tranquillity on the audience's faces made her unhappy. Straight away she could tell something that Ngoc had only just begun to realise. That they loved her. They loved her music, and they depended on her. Ngoc knew that they quite liked her, otherwise they wouldn't have come to see her so often, but she had little idea of the depth of their love.

But Ngoc's friend was not one to dwell on such things, and when this moment of reflection passed she began enjoying herself once more. A red Minsk drew up. She watched the men on it, and wondered if they were regulars. She cast her mind back and sifted through their conversation, trying to remember whether Ngoc had mentioned two Chinese-looking men with exceptionally greasy hair and identical moustaches. They were certainly looking over at Ngoc and passing comments to one another. No one else paid them any attention; they were just another part of the traffic.

They got off the bike and took down the big black case they had sandwiched between them. They kept looking and conferring, until at last they approached the crowd. Ngoc was oblivious, playing with her eyes closed and her head gently dancing to the sound of her own music. The men put the case at the foot of the steps and waited for her to finish.

All eyes were on them, and the piece was a long one. At first it seemed to go on for ever. They were impatient and wondered whether to prod her. Naturally, by the time she finished they were enraptured, and disappointed that the tune had come to an end. Ngoc looked up at them.

'This is for you,' said one of them, pointing at the case. 'A gift for you.'

Ngoc looked at the case and then back at the men. 'Who is it from?' she asked.

'We just deliver things,' said the other one. 'We don't know.' They both wanted to hear this very pretty girl play her new instrument, but their instructions were to leave it and go straight away.

As they got back on their bike and disappeared, everyone's eyes were on Ngoc. She could see it was a 'cello case, but who would have given her a 'cello case? She knew her old one was battered and about to lose one of its hinges, but who else would have noticed this and thought to replace it? She looked at her audience. Maybe one of them had given it to her. But how could they know it was her birthday? She spoke to them. 'What is this?'

If anyone knew where it had come from they were keeping it secret, because none of them replied and all their faces looked as surprised as hers. She approached it and looked for a message. There wasn't one. She put down her bow and unclipped the case to see if there was a clue inside.

Everyone watched in silence as she opened it and put her hand to her mouth in shock.

Inside lay the most beautiful 'cello she had ever seen.

V

Tuan could neither see nor hear, at least not in the way he had known these things before. His senses had merged into one, and even without the specifics of sight and sound he somehow managed to be aware of everything around him. He could feel. He could feel so much more than he could before. He had once read an article about sensory compensation; how soldiers blinded in battle had become accomplished musicians or piano tuners. He had lost his senses of sight, hearing, taste and smell, and these had been compensated for by an intensified sense of feeling. It went way beyond the physical sense of touch he had known before, and he could now feel everything. Everything was either knowledge or emotion; there was nothing else. So when Ngoc opened the case he knew it was her, he could feel it, and a strange sensation came over him. He felt his heart should be pounding like a water pump, as it had whenever he had been close to her before, but because he no longer had a heart he simply had an overwhelming sense of something. He didn't know what, but it was something incredible.

It was some time before Ngoc's shock subsided enough for her to take in the details of the 'cello. She looked at its grain, at its finish that was as flawless as her skin, and loved it. She took her old 'cello, the pitted, scarred 'cello she had loved for so long, put it gently back into its crumbling case and snapped shut the lid. Then, with everyone's eyes following her every movement, she reached down and touched her new one.

Tuan felt her fingers gently running up and down his body. She stroked him all over, enjoying his smoothness against her fingers but still too shocked to take him from the case. As she looked over him, her face was reflected in the sheen of the varnish, and he felt her beauty and her joy. He could not believe it. After so much waiting the 'cello girl was finally touching his body, and every movement of her fingers was like a thousand bursts of love.

She slipped her right hand around his neck and gently levered him up. She took her left hand, and lifted him out of his case. Then she put him into her playing position, cradled between her legs. She was still too stunned to play him and sat there, feeling the curves of his body with her fingers. He was where he had wanted to be for so long, and the bursts of love kept exploding inside him. He longed for her to play so that they could really merge into one. Just to have her touch him made everything worthwhile, but they would only be really united when she was playing and he was making heavenly music for her. Only then would they be a true, equal partnership.

She plucked the open strings, and was surprised to find that they were in tune. Perfectly in tune. She leaned over to get her bow, and as she did the neck of the 'cello brushed against her right breast. Tuan wondered why he didn't explode. She picked up the bow from the top step, and prepared to play. She took a moment to look at the faces around her and the traffic roaring by. Then she closed her eyes, positioned her fingers and the bow, and began.

Tuan's happiness was immeasurable. He sang for her, his body vibrated and sent out the notes her fingers asked for. Nothing else mattered to him. All that he had lost was nothing compared to what he had attained in his new life. As she played, he sang the happiest music imaginable.

But after a while Ngoc began to look uneasy. The look of bewildered joy drained from her face, and she frowned. Suddenly she stopped in the middle of the piece and everyone stared at her, wondering why. She never left a tune hanging in mid-air. She hadn't for as long as most of them had been listening to her. She looked at her friend. 'Enough for tonight,' she mumbled, and quickly bundled Tuan back into his case and slammed the lid shut.

Tuan felt as though he had been hit by a tram. To be at the pinnacle of happiness, only for it to end so suddenly was unbearable. He could not understand why she had stopped touching him, why he had so quickly been put back into his case.

'Let's go,' she said to her friend. Ngoc picked up her old 'cello case and made her way across the pavement. She gestured for her friend to follow, and as she did she picked up the new 'cello, which Ngoc had left lying by the steps and seemed to have forgotten about in her hurry. By the time her friend reached the roadside, Ngoc had hailed a taxi and was bundling her old 'cello in.

Ngoc spent the journey home looking silently out of the window, and as they got as far as the taxi could go down her alley she began, quietly, to cry. Her friend hugged her, but had no idea why Ngoc was acting as though she had suffered a terrible blow. Maybe it was all the excitement of the day. The birthday meal, the new 'cello. Perhaps it had all become too much for one day. They paid the driver more than they could really afford, and walked down the alley and back to the house, carrying a 'cello each in a silence broken only by Ngoc's sniffing.

The next morning Ngoc waited on Duong Dien Bien Phu for a xe lam to take her friend all the way over to Cholon bus station. They talked excitedly of a planned visit by Ngoc to Ben Tre Province before her course started.

'You must bring your 'cello and play for my husband,' said her friend.

Ngoc's face fell, and she looked away as she mumbled, 'Oh no. I don't think I could take it all that way. It's so old I don't think it would survive the journey. All that way on the bus and the boat.'

'Old? But it's brand-new. It looks strong enough to me.'

'But I was thinking of my other 'cello.'

'Well, whichever one you bring it would be nice to hear you play again.'

'Maybe.' There was a silence.

'What's wrong? Why were you crying last night?'

'Because it was all so strange. I couldn't play any more. The music had left me.'

'But it sounded fine to me, and to everyone else. Maybe you were tired after all the celebrations. That was a really pretty tune you were playing. Your new 'cello sounds so nice, so happy. You make such beautiful music together.'

'But that is just it,' said Ngoc. 'I wasn't playing a happy tune. I was trying to play a sad tune. It was a piece I had written about someone I used to know. It was supposed to be a very sad tune, and it just wasn't right for it to be so happy. It was supposed to be a moving piece, but it just sounded so happy. It was wrong. I tried to carry on but it was as though someone else was playing, not me. I wasn't in control.'

'Do you mean the 'cello was making the wrong notes?'

'No, they were all the right notes. Only they sounded so . . . happy. I can't think of another word. It was wrong. I don't know how to explain it.'

'Maybe . . .' but her friend couldn't offer her suggestion because a xe lam drew up and she leapt in. Ngoc waved her off, and walked back to her house feeling uncomfortable, as though someone had done something terrible to her, but she didn't know what it was.

The next day was Tuesday, and the xich lo waited for her in the alley. She never came. Instead she stayed at home reading her Viet-English dictionary, writing down some of her favourite words and wishing she knew how to say them aloud. The new 'cello lay by the front door, where it had been left by her friend on the Sunday night. Ngoc couldn't go near it. The sight of it made her feel ill, and later that evening she got one of her brothers to put it away in the same corner where she had found her old one. She had thought about taking her old 'cello to the steps, but she was still worried. What if that one sounded wrong as well? Maybe she just couldn't play any more. Maybe her music had left her. And what if the person who had given her the new one was there, waiting to hear her play it? How would they feel when she turned up with her damaged old instrument? They would think her ungrateful.

There seemed to be a thousand reasons why she should not go out, so she didn't. She stayed at home and studied.

Everyone went to the steps that night. The policeman was there. The three boys. Everyone. They crouched or stood waiting for her, and when she didn't turn up they just waited in silence. There was nothing to say. There was nothing to talk about, just a vacuum in their lives left by the girl, so no one spoke. At the point in the evening when she would usually have been going home they dispersed, hoping to see her on the Friday. They didn't. She stayed at home again, busying herself with work around the house and preparation for university.

Ngoc went to Ben Tre Province for four days. She didn't take her 'cello. She hadn't played a note since that night on the steps. Anyway, she might have had to buy extra tickets for it on the bus and ferry. That was her excuse. She had a wonderful time, and came back to the city a lot happier than she had been when she left. But she had lost her music completely. It just didn't float around in her mind as it had done before. She tried her hardest to forget that she had ever played, and moved on to her new life at university. She left her new 'cello in the corner, and covered the case with off-cuts of cotton cloth so she could try to forget it was there. So the handsome 'cello remained in its case. It was there for her brothers if they ever wanted to play it, but none of them had a single note of music in them. Lots of noise, but not a note of music.

Ngoc believed in ghosts. She was convinced that she had seen four of them in her life. Lost souls wandering around after dark. They were trapped in a world that barely existed, and were condemned to follow the same paths for eternity. They didn't belong anywhere, and were stuck in places where no one wanted them. She felt great pity for them.

However, ghosts were the last thing on her mind when, one Wednesday afternoon after an Economics lecture, one of the boys came up to her and asked her what she was doing at the weekend and whether she would like to go to Buu Long Mountain. He was tall, intelligent and extremely good-looking. For a moment she was stunned, amazed that he had asked her. Why her? Why not one of the other girls? He could ask any of them and they would agree. He was everyone's favourite. So, before he had a chance to change his mind she told him that she would love to go to Buu Long Mountain with him, and gave him her address.

As she cycled home she felt something she had never felt before, and knew it was love. And as she pedalled she started to hum a tune. It was one she had written just before she had stopped playing. She couldn't believe it. With her music back with her she sped down her alley, dashed for her old 'cello and, smiling, started to play. Tune after tune tumbled from her and bounced around the room to the delight of her family, who had no idea she had ever progressed beyond her early caterwauling. That night she forgot her college work, and played and played and played.

*

From the darkness of his case Tuan felt every note, and each one mocked his love for the beautiful girl. He sensed her new happiness, attained entirely without him. He felt nothing but pain.

Buu Long Mountain was much as Ngoc had expected, but that didn't stop it from being the best day of her life. On the way there she sat on the back of her boyfriend's motorbike and put her arms gently around his waist. On the way back she was squeezing him so hard he could barely breathe.

They finished their perfect day with an evening cruise around town and a coffee on Nguyen Hue. At one point they went down Ly Tu Trong, past the Library of Social Sciences. There was a small group of people collected around the steps, looking at an empty space where a pretty girl used to play her 'cello. They were all silently praying for her return.

Ngoc didn't notice them. She forgot to look. Instead she just held on to the man in front and fell deeper and deeper in love.

Glass Eyes

Coquettita lived with her young lover on a heart-shaped bed in a small clearing in the middle of the forest. She was kneeling on his chest and had just hit his left eyeball with the heel of her right hand.

He yelped, and squirmed with pain. It was a totally different feeling from the ones he had experienced during his boyhood kickings not so long before, and somehow more intense. She raised her hand and again brought it hard down on his eye, this time with increased violence. The feeling went a long way beyond pain. He felt numb all over.

'Out. Out. Out,' she croaked with escalating irritation, her time-ravaged vocal cords torn almost to shreds after so many hours of shouting the night before.

'Stop it,' he said, grabbing her wrist firmly but without hurting her. 'You'll never get it out if you just keep hitting it. And anyway,' he looked away, 'I'm still not sure I want it out.'

'Not sure? Not sure?' She climbed off his chest and, struggling free from his grip, gave his eye a final off-target whack. She sat on the side of the bed, looking at the ground with her shaking head in her hands, her body heaving with every sharp, furious breath. 'What do you mean you're not sure?'

'I'm not sure.'

'But we discussed it last night.'

'I know we did. But I never agreed.' He was surprised and hurt by his own angry tone. At least, he was fairly sure he hadn't agreed. He could have done for a moment; maybe a little, sympathetic nod of a head or a hand placed gently on a shoulder meant the same as agreeing. He didn't know. There were lots of things he didn't know.

'I need to think about it,' he said. 'I like having two eyes, that's all. I'm used to it. I'm sorry.'

'You will be sorry,' she growled, and struck out at him once more, missing his face by an inch as he rolled away just in time. She lunged and grabbed him, but he escaped and stood at a safe distance looking at her.

Coquettita was naked except for a string of pearls. He was naked too but with no one there to see them it didn't matter. And they were in love. People in love like looking at each other with no clothes on. But as he saw in her contorted face the unvanquishable desire to pluck out his left eye he began, tentatively, to question the uncon-ditionality of his love for her. For the first time in the six days since they had met, he felt the urge to hide his nakedness behind a tree or under some ferns. He was frightened. It began to feel, if not exactly wrong, then somehow not quite right. He even thought about putting his clothes back on, but they were in her box under the bed so he couldn't. He didn't like these feelings, or the dull throb they made in his head. This had been his first falling-in-love experience, and the first taste of falling-out-of-love left him reeling. He felt dizzy and couldn't move, speak or anything.

'I need a spoon,' she said. He didn't respond. 'A tea spoon. That'll get the little fucker out, no problem. Get me a spoon.'

He didn't. He couldn't. He wished she hadn't sworn. It was the first time he had heard her use language like that, and it hit him like a mallet. For the first few days she had been a fairytale princess. Perfection. Everything he had ever imagined a lover to be, everything he had ever dreamed of and never, not even for a moment, believed he would ever attain. In all the waking dreams that had taunted his loneliness she had been smooth and young, with hair of gold and lips that were a sultry smear across her unblemished face. But he was surprised by just how little Coquettita's age mattered to him. Theirs was a perfect love in spite of everything. At least it had been until the night before, when she had started on about the eye business. It had been the first real element of friction between them.

*

He hadn't even noticed it at first. He had loved her eyes. He could see how beautiful they must have looked when she was a girl, but that wasn't the only thing he loved about them. He loved the way they were right then, at that moment. Even though they were wrinkled, and there were little fleshy pockets hanging over her eyelids, she still carefully sculpted her eyebrows into skinny arches, and religiously blackened her lashes. But what he loved most of all about her eyes was their elusiveness. Coy turns of her head gave him only the slightest, tantalising glimpses of them. And anyway, when they first met he was so overcome by the sight of her clad in a ground-sweeping ermine cloak which nearly matched the silver of her hair, that it was a while before he began to notice details.

But on their first evening together, after the fur had been thrown to one side and they lay exhausted and entwined on the bed, he began to drink in little pieces of her body, each one giving him a brand-new reason to love her. She offered him her hands to touch and kiss, and for a moment he loved her for these alone. He marvelled at their smallness compared to his, their red, painted talons and the crumpled, almost transparent skin clinging to the fingers. He nuzzled his way up her arm and on to her neck, where he remained for an age, sucking lipfuls of loose skin into his mouth and gently feeling it with his tongue and teeth. He took care not to leave any marks, just little silvery patches of saliva which glowed for a while before disappearing into the warm air. Then he unwrapped himself and pulled back from her to get a full view of her face. Her long white hair had flown all over the place and obscured most of her features. He took immeasurable delight in sweeping these unruly locks away from her face, combing them back into some kind of order with his fingers, and carefully tucking any stray strands behind her ears. When the vista was finally free of these precious obstructions, he stroked her cheek and beheld the view. She smiled back at him. He brushed his fingers across the curves of her eyebrows and started loving her for her eyes; loving them more than he had ever loved anything.

As she looked unfalteringly back into his eyes he felt himself being pulled into her life, becoming a part of her, and wondering how he had managed to go from day to day without her in his life, and why he had bothered. He was so absorbed in these new feelings that he didn't even notice the crashing sound coming from a few yards away. It was nothing spectacular, probably just a pine marten landing on a bad branch. Coquettita, however, heard it and instinctively she glanced in the direction of the noise without moving her head. Within half a second she was looking straight back at her young lover's face, but she knew that he had noticed: her right eye had flicked towards the sound but her left eye had stayed fixed, staring emptily straight ahead. All the natural, radiant pink drained from her face, leaving the bright red paint on her cheeks and lips set awkwardly against an almost brilliant white background. She looked away.

Her young lover didn't say a word. He could feel her sadness, and knew how out of place it was in this perfect world he had discovered. So he pulled her close, curled up beside her and together they fell asleep, one fleshy mound in the starlight. To him, her glass eye was just another reason to love her.

The next morning Coquettita seemed to have forgotten all about it, and the following days flew by in an Arcadian haze. She grabbed her young lover by the hand and pulled him to all her favourite spots in her area of the forest, where they wrestled playfully and picked little green apples from the trees, and lay together in a contented silence, looking at each other, kissing and smiling.

For these few days, Coquettita did almost all of the talking, telling tales of her life and stories about things that she had seen and done in the places they visited. As she spoke her right eye sparkled, danced and laughed with the new joy she had found. Her left eye sat sullen and unmoving in its socket.

Her young lover was happy just to listen, and spoke only when he was asked a question. He felt he had so little to offer, as though he were a stranger in the world beside this woman of knowledge and experience. Everything he had seen or done in his tender years shrank into insignificance, as though his life had begun the moment he chanced upon her in her clearing and saw her sitting just a few feet away, on her bed and in her ermine, painting her face with her right hand and holding a little mirror in her left. He had stood watching for a long time, utterly ensnared by her rare beauty; he knew that her age should have rendered her a sea-witch in his young man's eyes, but she was a vision and he watched her with his heart thumping so hard that he wondered why she wasn't able to hear or feel it. But it wasn't until after she had put her make-up and mirror back in the box under her bed that she noticed him. He now realised why this was; he had been standing on her blind side. She hadn't appeared to be at all surprised by his sudden appearance. It was almost as if she had been expecting him. She gave a little smile, made herself comfortable in a way that allowed her cloak to slip open, showing her bare, white legs, and invited him to join her by gently patting the bed just to her right, where she could get a good, clear view of him. They kissed before either of them spoke. That, he thought, had been when his real life had begun.

On the fourth day she took him a few miles away to a crystal-clear pool with a little waterfall running into it. They bathed together in the cool water.

'This is my favourite place,' her voice sang through the still air. 'What do you think of it?'

'It's beautiful.' He had almost added, 'Like you,' but was glad that he hadn't.

There was a long silence. Eventually, Coquettita took both her young lover's hands in hers and looked away from him, at the waterfall and the stream of ripples it sent to lap against their bodies. She started to speak. 'You're . . .' she faltered. 'You know, you're not the first.'

Her young lover was not surprised. He had already considered and accepted the probability of his having predecessors. He had spent many hours lying awake by her slumbering body, listening to the music of her nocturnal wheezing and wondering how many others had been treated to these seraphic tunes. His immediate desire to find every one of them and tear out their throats was softened by her presence and, content in his new life, he decided to forget about them. She was his now, they were somewhere else, and all that was important was the present; the two of them being together. He didn't know what to say, but thought he should say something so she didn't think he was angry or upset.

'How many?' he asked, and the second he said it he wished that he hadn't. It seemed so irrelevant, and made it sound as though it were an issue.

'About eight hundred,' she said, still looking at the ripples on the water. 'I'm sorry.'

'There's no need to be.' And there wasn't. He felt like telling her that she had been his first, but he couldn't see the point. It was obvious. It must have been. So he just pulled her close and clung to her as he had done almost constantly since they had met, showing that he still felt the same as he had always done. At least it felt like always, he thought to himself.

She turned and smiled, looking straight at him at last. And during these perfect days, neither of them mentioned her glass eye.

On the evening of the fifth day, while they were draped together across the bed, Coquettita started to cry. For a moment her young lover's world turned upside down. He couldn't bear it. 'What's wrong?' he asked.

'Nothing,' she replied, and burst into more sobs and tears.

'It can't be nothing,' he said, running his hand along her arm.

'Why don't you just go?' She brushed him away. 'Go on. Just go.'

At this, he joined in the crying with tears of bewilderment. 'Why? What have I done?'

'Oh, don't. I know you'll leave me in the end, so let's get it over with. The longer we draw this thing out the uglier it'll be, so just save us both the trouble and go now.'

'I don't know what you're talking about,' he replied. He really didn't.

'You always leave me. Always,' she half whispered and half spluttered.

'But I love you,' he told her again. 'You know that.'

'Words, words, words, and I've heard them all before.'

'And I . . .' He could barely get these words she had also heard before out for all his sobbing and sniffing. 'I thought you loved me too.'

'I do love you. I love you more than anyone I've ever met. More than . . . anyone. And that's why you've got to go. Can't you see?'

'No.' He couldn't. It didn't seem to make sense. 'I don't understand.'

'Look,' she said, and slowly she lifted her clawed fingers towards her glass eye. With the forefinger and thumb of her left hand she pulled her lids apart, and with the nails from her right hand she flicked the eye out on to the bed. 'Now do you understand?' Her young lover didn't know what to say, so he shook his head. 'They leave me because I'm a one-eyed freak. You will leave me because I'm a one-eyed freak. Believe me, you will.'

'No I won't. I won't ever leave you,' he cried, but couldn't bring himself to look at her face with its hole where her eye should have been. He looked at the glass ball that was staring at nothing, and wished she would put it back in.

When she did he looked at her again. 'It doesn't make any difference to me. I thought you knew.'

She looked at him, and gave a hint of a smile. 'All right. I believe you. I believe that's what you feel now. But, sooner or later, you'll be sick of the sight of me. I look wrong. You can't stay with somebody who looks wrong. One day you'll go. You'll find someone with two eyes. Someone normal like you.'

She could not believe that his love was incorruptible.

'No, I'll never leave you. I promise,' he said.

'Words, words, words.' She pulled out her box from under her bed, and rummaged around with the occasional sniff.

'What are you looking for?' he asked.

'This,' she said, and showed him what she had found. It was another glass eye. 'I've always kept a spare. It's never been used.' She pressed it into his palm, and closed his fingers firmly around it. 'Now I want you to prove it.'

'Prove what?' He shivered, guessing what she was going to ask of him.

'What you've been saying. That you'll stay with me.'

'How? How can I? I've told you I will, what more do you want?' He was blinking hard, and kept rubbing his eyes with his thumbs as if sawdust had blown into them.

'Become like me. Know what it's like to be me. Know what it's like to be deformed.'

'You're not deformed,' he shouted. 'You're perfect. Even with your glass eye you're perfect.'

'No. No, I'm not. Listen: do you want to know me? I mean really know me.'

'Of course I do.'

'But you never will. How can you?'

'What do you mean?'

'Because you will never understand what it's like to be me. Seeing the world through one eye, having a useless glass ball in the other, and having everyone look at you all the time. You will never understand me. No one understands me.'

'But what difference does it make? I even like it. It's just another part of you, and I like it just as much as I like the rest of you. I love it.' He wished she would believe him. He didn't know how he could make her. He had no idea. He felt he had no idea about anything.

They sat in silence until it was broken by Coquettita. 'Give me your left eye,' she demanded, taking the spare eye back and holding it in the palm of her hand, 'and I'll give you this. Then we'll be the same and we'll have to stay together because no one else will have us. Either of us. Listen to me.' Her voice softened and she took his hands in hers. 'You can't have love without sacrifice. Every lover there has ever been has had to lose something they hold dear, to give up a part of what they are to the one they're with, and we're no different from anyone else; we're just an ordinary couple after all. Being with someone will always involve killing little pieces of yourself, having a clear-out, moving on. I know. I've killed so many little pieces of myself that there's hardly any of me left. Any of the me from when I was young and didn't know anything, like you. But it's the only way. You've got to do it. Then I'll believe that you love me, that you're not just saying it, that you really want to stay with me. It's the only way. And anyway,' she started to growl again, 'if glass eyes are so attractive, it'll hardly be the end of the world for you to have one, will it? If it's so insignificant, you won't really notice it, will you? And if you won't even make these tiny little sacrifices . . .'

He felt trapped and didn't know what to do. He couldn't think of anything to say. He had said everything he could, and didn't want to repeat himself. He didn't understand this need for sacrifice within the perfect romance; he just couldn't grasp it. He was exhausted by the whole episode, so he stretched out beside her, put his arm across her body, kissed her cheek, pulled her close, buried his face in her flesh and closed his eyes, hoping to wake up to find everything better. It wasn't long before he had fallen asleep.

He woke up the next morning to find his Coquettita kneeling on his chest and hitting his eye as hard as she could.

He stood still, looking at her. She was standing facing him

a few feet away. 'Just get me a fucking spoon,' she bellowed, using that word again. 'There's one in my box. Go on.'

He didn't respond. He could only stand and look as the life drained out of him. He wondered if she had been replaced by some kind of gargoyle. She looked the same as she had always looked; at least he couldn't put his finger on any real difference beyond the fury in her face, yet she seemed to have changed almost beyond recognition. He could not see the heavenly creature he had spent the preceding days falling in love with. In her place was a chronically wrinkled woman with far too much paint on her sour face. He saw the glass eye glaring at nothing, but it wasn't that which made him feel so alone. It was as much a part of her as it had always been. He had loved it before as a feature of her perfection, and now he squirmed at the sight of it because it belonged to this shouting old stranger. He didn't want her. He could feel every one of the cells in his body calling out for his princess. More than anything he had ever wanted, he wanted his Coquettita to rise out of the living ashes he saw before him and for everything to go back to normal.

He began to walk towards her, drawn not by his desire, but by his longing to recapture the spirit which had escaped her, to lure it back into its home. The closer he got, the more clearly he saw her imperfections; the crows' feet across her face and the folds of skin hanging from her body at awkward angles. He found her repulsive, but he didn't stop. He took her in his arms and kissed her face; lots of little hard-lipped pecks all over. He felt her tense body slowly relax, and she began to respond. Their mouths met, and he ran his tongue over the gummy gaps between her teeth as her hands wriggled their way through the hair on the back of his head. He felt nothing, and told her that he loved her.

She took his hand, led him back to the bed and they merged. For the first time, his mind was elsewhere. Being with her was not enough. And it all just fizzled out. There was no momentary visit to a euphoric plane, no point at which he lost track of his place in the universe, neither knowing nor caring which way the sky was or whether he would ever make it back to wherever it was he had been to begin with. Instead it all just finished, and they lay there. He couldn't look at her. 'I love you,' he said again, thinking that maybe saying it would make it true, and everything would be back to the way it had been before.

'I know,' she whispered softly. 'I know you do.' She wriggled free from his arms and began to rummage through her box. She brought out an old spoon and went back to her young lover's side. She gently stroked his hair. He was still looking away. With the thumb and forefinger of her left hand she prised his lids apart. He didn't stop her. They were swollen and discoloured from the beating they had been given. The spoon slipped in as though it had been designed for the job, but levering the eyeball out was more difficult than she had anticipated and took a few attempts. When it was halfway out, she clawed it with her nails and yanked it all the way. He hadn't shouted out or anything. He had just lain there with his face screwed up, quietly growling, biting his lip and twitching. She hated causing him all this pain. It hurt her to do it, but she knew there was no other way. The colour had left his face, and a stream of blood ran down his cheek. She didn't look at his eye once it was out, she just threw it over her shoulder and started to hunt around for a way of cleaning him up. She found a dock leaf, wet from the morning dew, and gently wiped his face before slipping the glass eye in.

Through all the pain he was thinking, almost believing, that when he opened his remaining eye his princess would be there looking down on him like an angel or something, and the old feelings would come back, sending bolts of passion through his whole body. It was a small sacrifice, really. It was nothing at all.

The time came to face his new world of half-darkness. He opened his eyes, and the one that worked settled upon the face that looked down at him. The face of a veiny old woman. She was smiling, and stroking his chest.

'See. I do love you,' he mumbled, hoping it would make a difference. But his words didn't set the world alight. They just dripped out of his mouth and made a mess on the bed.

Mademoiselle Arc-en-ciel

R

Jean-Pierre had made friends with Jean-Luc, his landlord, which always made things a little awkward around the first of the month. Still, Jean-Luc knew he would get his rent in the end and never said a word about it. When the small envelope appeared noiselessly on the kitchen table, usually around the fourth or fifth, the fog lifted and everything slipped back into place.

The part of the house they both liked best of all was the veranda. It had been the veranda which had decided it for Jean-Pierre. In fact he didn't even step over the threshold before looking Jean-Luc in the eye and telling him he had got himself a deal.

'Don't you want to see the inside first?' Jean-Luc had asked.

Jean-Pierre took one last look at the big wooden platform they were standing on, the little front yard with its patchy, colourless grass, and the clear view of the street. It was a bit like being on a throne. He shook his head, shook Jean-Luc by the hand and said no. He moved straight in.

He hauled his bag upstairs and into his room, which was really just a closet with a few hooks, a wooden chair, a narrow bed and a window so high you couldn't look out of it without climbing up. Without taking much notice of his new lodgings he grabbed the chair and dragged it down the stairs, through the door and on to the veranda. He sat down, took off his boots, stretched out his legs and felt he had lived there all his life.

'Can I get you a glass of wine?' asked Jean-Luc. 'Or a beer?'

'I think you can,' said Jean-Pierre with the kind of smile that doesn't need a s'il vous plaît to go along with it. 'One beer for me.'

Jean-Luc came back a minute later with two steaming bottles. The arm of his chair doubled as a bottle opener. He passed a beer to Jean-Pierre, who raised it in thanks and drank. He held it up and nodded appreciatively, as though it were a rabbit he had just shot.

They sat in silence, enjoying the warm, still evening. Jean-Luc didn't want to fire all the usual questions. Where are you from? What's your job? He would find all that out soon enough. There was no hurry. Why not just enjoy a quiet beer? Lord knows, if they were going to be living in the same house they should at least be able to sit down and enjoy a quiet beer together. And they did. They watched the sun go down over some big smoking chimneys a mile or so off to the west. They finished their beers, and Jean-Luc went inside to get some more. Steaming again.

'That's a good old refrigerator we've got in there,' said Jean-Pierre. 'It keeps things cold.'

Jean-Pierre passed Jean-Luc a cigarette, and they relaxed even more for a while, until Jean-Pierre began to lean forward, squinting at something in the half-light. Jean-Luc was looking too. It was a figure moving around outside the house across the street. A girl. She was wearing a red dress, and had wet hair hanging down her back. She had a nice silhouette. That was about all Jean-Pierre could make out. She knelt down and picked up something from the ground. She held it to her face and rubbed it against her cheek. It must have been a little cat. She went back in.

'Who was that?' asked Jean-Pierre.

'Oh, that was Mademoiselle Arc-en-ciel. She lives across the street.'

'She's pretty.'

'Yes. She's a fine woman.'

'She is. She's a fine woman.'

They had another beer before turning in. Both of them had a warm feeling inside.

0

Jean-Pierre settled in over the next few days. He filled the refrigerator with beer for the two of them and put a few cheap bottles in the wine rack. He worked out how to light the grill, had a shower and a shave, and generally laid down his scent.

Every night they sat in their places on the veranda and drank a few beers or a bottle of wine as the sun went down. Occasionally Jean-Luc brought out plates of boring cuisine jeune homme that filled their bellies without them really noticing that they had eaten. They gradually began to find out little details about each other, one at a time. People they knew; some jobs they'd done; things they'd shot; each other's birthdays. They were about the same age. Still reasonably young, but neither of them had a job at the time. Jean-Luc was due to start one in town before long, pushing a pen for someone his uncle knew. He wasn't in a great hurry to start. He had Jean-Pierre's rent money to tide him over. Jean-Pierre was looking, but wasn't in too much of a hurry either. He had enough money to last him a while. Still, most days he would make the short walk into town and ask around. Meet people. Drink coffee. Sit around in the square making friends.

When Jean-Pierre was out of the house, Jean-Luc would go down into the cellar to play his trombone. He didn't like anyone to hear him play, and the basement muffled the sound pretty well. He had been teaching himself for a couple of years and knew a handful of tunes, but had never played in front of anybody. He was waiting for the right moment. The right audience. He never spoke about his trombone to Jean-Pierre, but Jean-Pierre knew about it. Sometimes on the veranda Jean-Luc, without knowing it, would hum a tune with his left fist pressed against his lips and his right sliding up and down in front of him. Jean-Pierre knew a trombone player when he saw one.

One night they were sitting on the veranda as usual, and using their tongues to pick awkward lumps of bread from between their teeth. Jean-Luc had just told Jean-Pierre how he had come to own the house.

'I suppose it's sad when your Grandma dies,' said Jean-Pierre. 'But getting a house must have softened the blow a little.' That should have sounded bad, but somehow it didn't.

Out of nowhere, a breathless Mademoiselle Arc-en-ciel came running up the path. She clung on to the wooden pillar and caught her breath. 'Did any of you two boys see mon petit minou?' she asked.

'Oh, er ... No, Mademoiselle Arc-en-ciel. I'm really sorry, but I've not seen her at all, Mademoiselle Arc-en-ciel,' said Jean-Luc. 'I'm sorry.'

'Oh dear. I don't know where she's got to.' She bit her

bottom lip. Her long wet hair was pulled back with a thick orange band. 'She's never run away before.'

'Don't you worry, Mademoiselle. We'll help you look,' volunteered Jean-Pierre, rising to his full height. 'We'll find your petit minou for you.' They both hopped down on to the lawn and the search began. Mademoiselle Arc-en-ciel ran off without a word. She was frantic.

Jean-Pierre and Jean-Luc had a quick look around the yard, then went into the street. It looked as though Mademoiselle Arc-en-ciel had got just about everyone out of their houses and joining in the search. There were people everywhere, looking under cars and shrubs, whistling, making kissing noises and gently tapping pet-food tins with forks.

From the distance came a man's voice. 'Mademoiselle. Mademoiselle Arc-en-ciel. Where are you, Mademoiselle Arc-en-ciel? I've got something for you. A surprise.' They couldn't see what was happening, but it sounded like a reunion. Some way down the street Mademoiselle Arc-en-ciel laughed, and it rang through the air like wind-chimes. They caught a glimpse of her as she ran into her house with a furry bundle clutched beneath her chin. She closed the door behind her. Gradually the street cleared. Everyone went back into their homes, and Jean-Pierre and Jean-Luc went back on to the veranda to finish their half-full bottles of beer.

'She's always washing her hair,' said Jean-Luc. 'Always.'
'Really?' said Jean-Pierre. He hadn't seen her close to
before.

Y

A fortnight later they were sitting on the veranda in the early evening, this time swilling stubborn chunks of meat from barely accessible regions of their gums with cheap but passable wine, when they saw Mademoiselle Arc-en-ciel heading towards them with a stack of envelopes in her hand. 'Good evening Mademoiselle Arc-en-ciel,' said Jean-Luc, and flushed a little.

'And a very good evening to you too, Monsieur Jean-Luc,' she said with a smile and a playful little curtsy. She fumbled with the envelope on the top of the pile, taking care not to drop the whole lot. It was unsealed, and with her tongue touching her top lip in concentration she wrestled a greetings card out. It had on it a picture of a window with a vase of flowers on the sill. She turned to Jean-Pierre. 'I'm sorry, but I don't know your name. We haven't been introduced.' She looked at Jean-Luc and twitched her nose, but didn't really mean it.

'You can call me Jean-Pierre, Mademoiselle Arc-en-ciel.'

She smiled, put her tongue back on her top lip and fumbled in her cardigan pocket for a pen. 'Oh,' she said, looking disappointedly at what she found. 'I'm sorry, but you'll have to be in pencil. I thought I had my pen with me. I must have left it in the house.'

Jean-Luc wondered how many pens and pencils she had in her house.

When she had finished writing Jean-Pierre's name in the card, she tucked her pencil behind her ear and slid the card back into the envelope, which she then carefully licked and sealed. She got hold of her pencil again, and neatly wrote Jean-Pierre's name on the envelope. He watched her closely. Her hair was dry for once. It had a slight wave to it and looked very nice, but there were a couple of little flecks of scalp around her parting. Not enough to worry about, just one or two. Jean-Luc didn't even notice them.

'You want to be careful wearing pretty little shoes like that in a dusty old street like this, Mademoiselle Arc-en-ciel,' he said. Her yellow pumps had become discoloured around the soles.

'Oh, I don't worry too much about that,' she replied, dotting the i. 'They're just shoes. They get me around.' She darted up on to the veranda, through the gap between their chairs, and pushed the envelope under the door, which was half open anyway. 'I think the postman's been, boys,' she cried and, smiling to herself, she ran down the path and to all the other houses in the street, dropping off cards as she went.

They watched her until she was out of sight. Sometimes she would stop for a bit of a talk, and other times she wouldn't. Jean-Luc went in and got the card. The envelope read: 'To Monsieur Jean-Luc and Monsieur,' then in pencil, 'Jean-Pierre.' He tore it open, took the card out and looked at the picture of the window and the vase of flowers for a while. He opened it and read aloud. 'Dear Monsieur Jean-Luc and Monsieur,' then in pencil, 'Jean-Pierre.' Then back to pen. 'Thank you for helping me to look for mon petit minou the other day. She is back at home again now and promised me never to run away again! Best Regards, Arc-en-ciel.' There was a little pencil x by her name.

Jean-Pierre asked to see it, and Jean-Luc passed it across. He looked for a while before putting it back in the envelope. 'That's nice,' he said.

'Yes,' agreed Jean-Luc. 'She's a nice lady.'

'Yes.'

Later they caught a glimpse of her as she dashed back into her home empty-handed. They drank on, neither saying a word. They were both too busy thinking about that little x.

G

Jean-Luc had the score for several tunes, and had learnt some of them well enough to be able to play them without having to read the notes. He was almost ready to play in front of someone. Down in the cellar he blew his way through 'J'Aime Bien Ton Visage Ce Soir', and 'Je Me Sens Comme Ça Aujourd'hui'. They were nearly perfect. He felt a little nervous, knowing what he would have to do once he had got them just right. With his heart in his mouth, he drained the moisture from the trombone into the pot of his cactus, put it back in its case and went up on to the porch to wait and see if Jean-Pierre had got them any food.

He waited for an hour or two before Jean-Pierre came into view, holding a brace of hares by their ears in one hand and his shotgun in the other. As he got closer, Mademoiselle Arc-en-ciel appeared from her house carrying a watering can. She was wearing a green towel haphazardly scrunched around her head. There were strands of wet hair springing out from obscure gaps at oblique angles. She saw Jean-Pierre. 'The hunter returns,' she called, and looked admiringly at the hares. 'I think you need a lady to skin those for you,' she said.

'Oh, we're all right Mademoiselle Arc-en-ciel. Jean-Luc's a real old professional with a knife. He'll have these babies in the pot in the blinking of an eye. Maybe even sooner.'

'Well, don't say I didn't offer,' she called, lifting herself up on to the balls of her feet to pour a few drops of water on to a weary-looking hanging basket and going back inside.

Jean-Pierre stepped back up on to the porch, dropped the hares on the floor by Jean-Luc's feet and sat down.

'You should have let Mademoiselle Arc-en-ciel skin those for us,' said Jean-Luc. 'It would be nice to have her around.'

'She was only joking,' said Jean-Pierre. 'She doesn't want to come over here.'

'I don't know. Maybe she needs a little company. I think she's shy.'

'Maybe.'

'It's just her and her mother in that big old house.' He shook his head. 'And the cat. I forgot the petit minou. She used to have a friend come and take her out for the evening in his car. But that hasn't happened for a long time now. Not since before you came.'

'Oh.'

'Yes, I'm going to get her to come over.'

'How?' asked Jean-Pierre.

'I'll think of a way.' He picked up the hares from the floor and took them through to the kitchen. He hung one for another day and dealt with the other on the chopping board. Within a few minutes it was in the pot, sending what little scent it had around the house and out on to the veranda.

B

Jean-Luc spent part of his first month's wages on a nanny goat. He pulled her home from the farm on a rope, and tied her to a pole in the middle of the lawn. She ate just about all of the scraggy grass more or less straight away. 'You've got an appetite on you, my friend,' he said to her, and realised he would have to go and get some goat food before too long.

Jean-Pierre wasn't home. He hardly ever came home before the evening. He had the occasional day's work, usually just helping somebody out, but even when he wasn't working he would go and see what was happening in town and drink coffee, or go into the fields with his gun. Anything but sit around the house with nothing much to do.

Jean-Luc was surprised by just how quickly his bait worked. He hadn't been home more than half an hour when Mademoiselle Arc-en-ciel streaked across the street with a yelp of delight. 'Oh, you've got yourself a little goat,' she cried, and running up to her, tried to give her a stroke.

The goat, nervy from the day's upheaval and unused to screaming people charging at her, backed off, reached the end of her rope, jerked to a halt and fell awkwardly on to her side. Mademoiselle Arc-en-ciel was distraught. She put her hand to her mouth and said, 'I'm sorry. Oh, I'm so sorry. I didn't mean to . . .'

'Don't worry, Mademoiselle Arc-en-ciel,' said Jean-Luc.

The goat quickly untangled her legs and got back on her feet, looking a little dazed but unhurt. 'I'm sure it's nothing personal.' He went up to the goat and, cautiously, petted her. She seemed uncomfortable, and flicked her head around, but she didn't run away.

'Come here,' he said to Mademoiselle Arc-en-ciel.

She approached and reached out her hand. She gently touched the goat on the head. It looked a little bewildered, twitched and took a couple of steps to the side. She began to stroke first its head, then its neck. Jean-Luc stood a few paces back and watched as Mademoiselle Arc-en-ciel crouched down, her little fingers running softly up and down the goat's coat. It appeared to be calming down.

'What's his name?' she asked quietly, turning to Jean-Luc.

'It's, er . . . It's a lady goat.'

'Oh, I'm sorry.' She laughed, and it rang through the air like wind-chimes. 'What's her name, then?'

'She doesn't have one. Not yet anyway. Any ideas?'

'Oh, let me think.' Her tongue touched her top lip in concentration. 'How about Hélène?'

The goat seemed to take exception to this. At the mention of the name, she bit on the arm of Mademoiselle Arc-en-ciel's sweater. The evenings were getting colder, and everyone had started wearing sweaters. Mademoiselle Arc-en-ciel pulled to get free, but Hélène's jaws were like clamps. Jean-Luc intervened, grabbing the sweater with both hands and pushing the goat away with his left boot. After a quick struggle and a soft tearing sound, the battle was over. Hélène had retreated as far from them as her rope would allow, and had a clump of blue wool hanging from her mouth.

'Cannibal,' joked Mademoiselle Arc-en-ciel, surveying the hole in her sleeve.

'I'm sorry about that, Mademoiselle Arc-en-ciel. I had no idea I'd gone out and got myself a crazy killer for a pet.'

'It doesn't matter. It's only an old thing.' It didn't look old to Jean-Luc. He was sure he had never seen it before, and thought that it suited her very well.

'Well, I suppose this is the first and last time you'll be coming to see my new friend the goat,' he said, believing it.

'No way. I'm sure me and . . . Hélène,' she lowered her voice to a whisper when she said the name, 'will get along fine. We've had a bit of a rocky start, but now she knows who I am, and that I've got you on my side, we'll be able to make a go of it.' She turned to the goat. 'Won't we?' Hélène looked sheepish.

'Well,' said Jean-Luc, 'you come any time you like. I'm sure . . .' He started to whisper, 'Hélène . . . will be looking forward to it. Won't you?' They both laughed, and Hélène skulked.

Jean-Pierre came through the gate, home from wherever

it was he had been. 'Oh,' he said. 'Looks like we've gone and got ourselves a goat. What's his name?'

Jean-Luc and Mademoiselle Arc-en-ciel looked at each other conspiratorially, and whispered in unison, 'Hélène.' They laughed, and Jean-Pierre went inside to get something to drink.

I

Jean-Pierre had got himself fixed up with a load of late-shifts, so the veranda wasn't getting as much use as it had done. And anyway, the weather was so cold you had to wrap yourself up like a mummy just to go outside, and the ice-cold beer had lost its appeal.

Jean-Luc came home from work late in the afternoon, and leaned his bicycle against the veranda. The house was empty and he made his way straight down to the cellar. He unclipped the trombone's case, assembled it, and was about to start playing when he noticed that the mouthpiece was damp, as if he had only just finished playing it, and hadn't wiped it clean. He had never known that to happen before. He tried to work out when he had last played it. Two nights before. Or was it three? Whatever, he felt sure he could remember draining all the water. It was strange that it should still have spit on it after all that time, and strange that he had packed it away like that in the first place. Still, he had a lot on his mind. Maybe he hadn't drained it after all. He hadn't been paying the best attention to a lot of things lately. He gave it a wipe on the sleeve of his jacket, pressed the cold brass to his lips and played. Perfectly. Beautifully. He slipped in to the key change at the end of 'C'est Pourquoi Je Te Regarde' like it was second nature, and a shiver ran down his back. He hadn't read a note of music or made a single mistake for two weeks. The time had come.

He made himself a coffee and walked over to the front door, with his mug in one hand and his trombone in the other. He balanced the coffee on his knee and flipped the latch. He sat down, put his trombone on the floor in front of him and sipped his drink. He watched the steam rising from it, and the clouds his breath made in the moonlight.

Mademoiselle Arc-en-ciel had made it her habit to visit the goat almost every evening, and this night he sat there in his coat and gloves, waiting for her to come over and pet Hélène and pass the time of day.

Waiting for her to notice the trombone and exclaim that she didn't know he played.

Waiting for her to ask him to play her a tune and for her to not take a modest 'no' for an answer.

He waited for her to come up on to the veranda, sit across from him on Jean-Pierre's chair and ask him to play another, and then another.

He waited for her to listen to the music and to look at her old friend Jean-Luc as though she had just seen a smiling angel at her window.

He waited for her to ask him to walk her home and for them to kiss in the shadows by her front door, quietly so her mother wouldn't know.

He waited.

He finished the coffee, and got colder and colder. He lit a cigarette and carried on waiting. Suddenly, Mademoiselle Arc-en-ciel's door opened. At least it seemed sudden to Jean-Luc; in fact it opened quite normally. There she was, like an indigo puffball in her huge jacket and with her hair all tucked up inside her woolly hat. Jean-Luc's heart raced, and he stubbed out the cigarette with the toe of his boot. She went out into her garden and knelt down. In seconds she was back in the warm, clutching her petit minou in her gloved hands. Jean-Luc let out a groan and looked at his trombone, shaking his head as though it were the instrument's fault.

He was about to go back inside and start getting some food going for when Jean-Pierre came home, when Mademoiselle Arc-en-ciel's door opened again. This time she came straight out and headed towards him. He started to shake a little, and his throat went dry. She came in to the garden.

'Good evening, Jean-Luc,' she said with a smile.

'Good evening, Mademoiselle Arc-en-ciel.' He was surprised by just how calm he sounded to himself.

'Good evening, Hélène.' She went over and hugged the goat. They had patched up their differences and were now the best of friends. 'How are you tonight? Cold? Is that nasty man making you stay out in this weather? How could he?' She smiled and turned to Jean-Luc. She noticed the trombone lying by his feet.

'Hey, whose is that?'

'Oh, it's mine,' he replied, as casual as anything.

'I didn't know you played an instrument.'

'Well, you know.' He shrugged. 'I play around with a couple of tunes. I'm nothing special.'

'I bet you are,' she replied. 'I always wished I could play something. I tried the piano once, but . . . no.'

This was not in the script, but Jean-Luc stayed in control. 'Oh, I'm sure you could play if you practised.'

'No.' She went back to stroking the goat. 'No, not me. I'm not musical like you.'

'How do you know I'm musical? You've never even heard me play.'

'Oh, I can just tell you are. Hey, why don't you play me a tune?'

Jean-Luc's heart was reaching bursting point. 'Oh, no. I couldn't.' He was itching to reach down and grab the freezing brass.

'Well you suit yourself, but be warned: one day I'll get a tune out of you, Monsieur Jean-Luc.' She stood up. 'I'll see you soon. Au revoir, Hélène.' Giving the goat one last pat on the head, she was off. Jean-Luc kicked himself very hard in the left shin with the heel of his right boot.

He went inside and did things around the kitchen. He wasn't really concentrating. All he could think of was Mademoiselle Arc-en-ciel, and every word of their conversation. Particularly his coy, stupid little refusal.

Jean-Pierre came in from work just as the tasteless food was ready. They ate it at the kitchen table and forced it down with red wine. Neither of them said much. Jean-Pierre went to bed first, and Jean-Luc went to lock up. As he bolted the front door, he realised his trombone must still be lying on the veranda. He went out to get it. It was right there where he had left it. Jean-Pierre must have walked straight past it on his way in, but he hadn't said a word. It was almost as if he was used to it being around.

V

Jean-Luc didn't mention the trombone at the breakfast table, and neither did Jean-Pierre. Jean-Luc thought he might as well forget about it. After all, Jean-Pierre wasn't the greatest observer he had ever known, and anyway the trombone wasn't a secret any more. It had made its debut. But before, he had only ever thought of Mademoiselle Arc-en-ciel when he had been practising. He had never given a thought to anyone else hearing him play, or even knowing that he played. The thought of Jean-Pierre knowing about it felt strange, but if he'd seen it, he'd seen it. It didn't really matter.

Jean-Pierre cleaned his plate and took his gun down from its rack. 'I'm off to shoot something,' he said.

'Have you got any work today?' asked Jean-Luc.

'Well, I think I'll be moving some geese around this afternoon. If I do I'll be a hungry man, so don't forget about me.'

'I won't, I won't. Just so long as you get us something tasty.'

'I'll do my best. Have a good day.' He was off.

'See you later,' said Jean-Luc. He had enough time for a shave. Then he went, through the bitterly cold morning, to work.

Apart from the money, the only thing Jean-Luc really

liked about his work was that his department was in a room right in the middle of the building, and had no windows. So, whenever the power packed up it was too dark to work and he would be sent home on full pay. It had only happened once before in the three months he had been there, and then it had been only twenty minutes before the end of the day. This time though, the big-freeze took its toll at twenty past one in the afternoon. The lights snapped out, and Jean-Luc stopped in mid-sentence and laid down his pen. Everyone fumbled their way into the light of the street and hung around in their coats, hoping that nothing could be done to save the day. It couldn't, and after twenty minutes of chugging false-starts the generator convinced them that it wasn't going to work, and they were told to come back as usual the following morning to see if everything had returned to normal.

So he cycled home, thinking about what he was going to say to Mademoiselle Arc-en-ciel if she came over to see the goat that night, and hoping he would finally get to play for her. He had never felt so ready.

He got home and found three rabbits in a pile on the kitchen table. Jean-Pierre had evidently had a good morning. Jean-Luc thought he could use the free time to start getting them ready for the table. For Jean-Luc, skinning a rabbit was almost meditation. It needed so little thought. He had been helping his grandpa with his rabbits since he could be trusted not to cut himself, and one of the first things he had bought with Jean-Pierre's rent money was a good solid knife with a lethal blade which he kept sharpened like a razor.

He took the first rabbit, slapped it on the chopping board and cut off its feet with four expert flicks. Without really concentrating, he scored a shallow line along the length of its belly. He was dreaming of Mademoiselle Arc-en-ciel. They were walking down the street, hand in hand. They were laughing quietly at the looks on people's faces as they saw them together and realised. He slipped the knife under the rabbit's skin and wriggled it just enough to separate it from the meat. He laid it down for a moment, and carefully eased the skin over the hind legs. As he worked he began to hum the melody of one of his favourite tunes, 'Une Petite Demoiselle Precieuse Qui S'Appelle "Toi" '. His trombone was singing in his head. His favourite trick was to get the rabbit's head off in one length of the blade. He lifted the knife and brought it down fast. This time he only got about half a centimetre into its neck, probably because he wasn't really thinking about it. He pulled the knife along and down, and was hardly more than halfway through by the time the tip of the blade slipped on to the board. He sawed the rest of its head off, and threw it along with the feet and skin into the wooden box they used for waste. He was sitting by the sea, looking out to the horizon with his arm around Mademoiselle Arc-en-ciel as he sank the knife into the rabbit's shining belly. She tilted her head and rested it on his shoulder. The blade slipped through the strong, young flesh as though it were Camembert. He scooped out its innards, put the heart, liver and kidneys aside to boil up later, and threw the rest into the box. By the time he was cutting along the length of the rabbit's spine, he and Mademoiselle Arc-en-ciel were up to their knees in the sea. Giggling, she splashed him. He cut off its legs at the joints, and threw them away. They landed on the dead, staring head. He was shaken a little from his dreams by having to choose which rabbit to deal with next. He couldn't see much of a difference, so he chose the one on top and, still humming, skewered it right through its head with the knife and picked it up to bring it over to the chopping board.

It slipped gracelessly from the blade, leaving a smear on the steel and making a thud on the board. As it did, he noticed that even though he had stopped humming for a moment, the tune had carried on. He froze where he stood, with his mouth slightly open and the knife in his fist. Where was it coming from? Who was playing it?

A wrong note shook him alive, and his eyes darted around as he listened to find out what was going on. He followed the sound into the hallway. He stopped and listened again. There was another wrong note, and a pause, then the song resumed. It was coming from upstairs. Quietly and slowly he climbed the stairs, listening to every note with the knife still clutched in his hand, his heart pounding irregularly, as if fireworks were going off in his chest.

It was coming from Jean-Pierre's room. There was a trombone playing in Jean-Pierre's room. It was his trombone. He knew it. He didn't know how, but he could tell. He paced across the landing and stood a few feet away from the door. His breath was coming in sharp, trembling gasps. The trombone hit a note that was so far off that the whole tune collapsed. This must have been funny, because someone in the room laughed, and it rang through the air like wind-chimes. Tears filled Jean-Luc's eyes, and ran in rivers down the guttering on each side of his nose and into the corners of his mouth. He wiped them away with the back of his hand, nearly cutting a chunk out of his face as he did so. He heard some more sounds. Jean-Pierre was laughing quietly. Then he started to speak. Jean-Luc could hear everyword through the flimsy door.

'Do you want a go?' he asked.

'Oh, I don't know,' said Mademoiselle Arc-en-ciel. 'I'm sure it's not as easy as it looks.'

'Oh, it is. Go on.'

'All right. Give it here.' There was a sharp intake of breath, followed by a low, ugly squelch. She dissolved in giggles. Then there was a short silence, followed by two voices making the content 'mmmmmm' sound, almost like a cat purring. He had heard people make that sound before. He had sometimes even made it himself when there had been no one in the house to hear him. The tears carried on.

'Hey, Arc-en,' said Jean-Pierre, 'shall I play you another?'

'No, not now,' she replied.

'Why not? Don't you like my playing?' Jean-Pierre was pretending to be a little hurt and indignant. Jean-Luc's pain intensified. As he stifled his sobs, his face contorted and he looked like an ugly baby.

'No, I like it well enough. It's just . . .'

'Just what?'

'It's just it's cold and I need someone to warm me up, that's all.'

'Oh do you? Then you should go and find someone,' said Jean-Pierre.

'But I'm too cold to move. I can't look far.'

'Well, just this once I suppose I'll help you out, but don't you go taking me for granted.'

'You're so kind to me, you really are.'

There was another silence, but this time it didn't end. It was broken only by the thud of the trombone falling from the bed on to the wooden floor.

Jean-Luc's shock and sadness started to turn to anger. Arc-en. Arc-en? How could he call Mademoiselle Arc-en-ciel 'Arc-en'? How could she let him? He spun the knife around in his stained fingers. How could she sit there and listen to the rubbish Jean-Pierre was playing on his trombone? The silence tore through him. He couldn't stand it. He couldn't stand the thought of Jean-Pierre feeling Mademoiselle Arc-en-ciel's body through her dress. Her pretty violet dress. He knew she would be wearing her violet dress, the one she had always worn as she waited by the gate for the car to come and take her away for the evening. Undoing the buttons down the front, slipping his hand inside and touching her soft skin with his rough hands. And her letting him do it. How could she let him do that to her?

He began to move without making a sound. He padded across the landing and back to the top of the staircase. He went gently down the stairs, across the hall and into the kitchen. He put the knife on the chopping board, next to the skinned rabbit. Then he left the house, crossed the veranda, walked past the goat and into the street. He kept on walking. Away from the house and away from the town. Away from everything he had ever known. Without once looking over his shoulder, and with tears dripping from his chin and melting the frost on the ground, he walked into the freezing afternoon.

Landfill

First

After the council took away his bins he had to break into the landfill site to get rid of his rubbish. He compressed about a fortnight's dead wood into a hessian sack, and carried it into the night. The welkin's luminescence lit his journey through the deserted streets, across the disused aqueduct and to the high wire fence that marked his destination. It was at least four times his height. Looking through to the other side he saw a band of grass several yards across before the waste began. He hadn't remembered it from his previous trips to the periphery of the site, and realised that there was no way he could execute his original plan to scramble to the top of the fence and empty the sack straight into the dump. He would have to climb right over, cross the grass and leave the rubbish within the defined inner perimeter. Otherwise, come the morning, his isolated waste would be found and possibly traced. He could see no real alternative.

With the sack in his right hand he gripped the wire and climbed, struggling to get his boots into the barricade's small diamonds. When he neared the top he was able to haul the sack over, and it thumped on to the grass. In moments he was over the top and scrambling like a squirrel down the inside. He leapt the last few feet and landed by the sack. He picked it up and hauled it over to where the recently mown grass ended and the rubbish began.

He walked into the leavings for a couple of minutes, watching his boots as they trampled broken glass, household leftovers, builders' waste, plastic sacks with concealed contents and just about every other class of refuse. He stopped, dropped the sack on to the debris and looked around. Floodlit by the stars, the scene was almost entirely monochrome. For a moment he thought himself a detail in a fading photograph, and was glad he had climbed right in. He absorbed the atmosphere for a while longer before untying the sack, kicking it over, heaving it upside down and emptying it. Seven rats the size of baby badgers streaked on to the scene, and began to eat what they could of his kitchen scrapings. Startled by this intrusion, he quickly turned to leave.

By the edge of the tip, where the grass began, he saw the silhouette of a figure standing still and looking in his direction. His heart almost exploded, and he jerked to a halt and froze. Instinctively, he dropped the empty sack.

Someone must have called the guard. He felt his insides cramp as he searched for a solution. He turned and looked behind him. There was nothing but rubbish as far as he could see. If he ran away he would almost certainly be found at daybreak after a miserable night with the rats. Reluctantly, he chose to walk towards the guard and present himself.

As he neared, he saw that the figure was a girl. A small female guard with thick black hair that reached her knees. When he got close enough to see her clearly, he realised that she was not a guard after all. Instead of a uniform, she was wearing as a dress a large man's pin-striped suit jacket. It was torn, frayed and dirty and its buttons were gone. It was wrapped around her otherwise naked body and held in place by her hugging arms.

'Hello,' she said, sadly. 'I am Maria.'

He was dazzled. He had never seen anyone quite like her, and wondered from which hemisphere her blood had come. Her pale blue eyes shone from her dark brown face into the leaden night, her hair hung absolutely still against her long bare legs, and her jacket-dress revealed a suggestion of a celestial bosom. She pulled her clothing tighter, and answered the question that was emblazoned across his face before he could summon the courage to ask it.

'My great-grandparents were Patagonian, Ethiopian, Amerindian, Polynesian, Micronesian, Polack, Scouse and

Eskimo.' Her brow crumpled, her eyes became too sad for the world, and it was clear that her burden far outweighed that of Atlas. She looked beyond the distance, and sighed. 'That is why I am so beautiful.'

Having no idea how to respond he passed her, crossed the grass, climbed over the fence and walked back to his flat with her image branded deep into his cerebral retina.

Landfill

Second

When he slept he dreamed of her, and when he opened his eyes a vision of her was waiting for him. All day he thought of nothing else. His concentration evaporated and he tripped over paving stones, smashed into door jambs and was unable to utter even the simplest sentence without drifting into unintelligible mutterings. He knew exactly what it was that had charged into his life and poured itself into every crevice of his body and mind. He wanted to bury his face in her hair. He wanted to be kind to her.

The sun taunted him with its presence as he waited for the night and a chance to go back to the landfill site. It seemed to hang in the sky far longer than usual, creeping like an old woman hoping for alms. As dusk arrived his fear grew. He could not be certain that she would be there. There was no reason why she should be. And if she was there, what would he say? He ran through the list of things to talk about that he had been working on all day, and each item sounded totally inappropriate. Still, he had to go. He knew that he had no choice. He was in love, and no longer his own master. As the time came his love for her pushed him out of his flat and frog-marched him, terrified, towards the landfill site. As he crossed the aqueduct he considered jumping from it to his death rather than face her rejection, but love held him firmly in its grip and drove him forward to the woman it had chosen.

Suddenly, as he climbed down the inside of the site's fence, he forgot what she looked like. His every pore opened, and he wondered if he would recognise her. Her face had been before him all day, but now it had vanished. She became a blur, and the chilling feeling that he would not recognise her if he saw her shot through him. He couldn't remember her name, either. As he stood alone on the grass he suddenly felt ungainly and plain. He wanted to go home before things got even further out of control, but love had annexed his reason, and it bullied him into waiting around to see if she turned up. He walked on into the rubbish, taking the same route as he had the night before and hoping he wouldn't see those rats again. He became entangled in the inner tube of a child's bicycle and fell forward. He landed at an awkward angle and gashed his cheek on a rusty shard of metal.

Immediately he felt a hand at his elbow, pulling him back up on to his feet. Through his daze he could tell that it was the person he had come to find, and as the blood poured from him he felt stupid for having fallen over. She tore a piece from the sheet of surgical gauze she was wearing as a toga, and started to clean him up.

'Oh, I think you are a poor thing. How do you feel?' He couldn't place her accent.

'Fine, fine. I can hardly feel it.' The wound was stinging so much he had tears in his eyes and could barcly see. She used these droplets to help clean the blood from his skin and the grains of rust from his wound. As she dried the remaining drops from his eyes he was able to see her clearly. Her beauty nearly knocked him over, and he felt his legs begin to buckle at the realisation that she was a lovely, caring person as well as a beautiful one. Again, the words he considered saying to her sounded pathetic, and he saw no reason why someone like her should listen to a single syllable he said.

'Are you sure you are well? That was a nasty fall. I saw it. I was watching you all the time, even as you climbed over the fence.' He was sure her face was even sadder than it had been the night before, and he desperately wanted to touch her cheeks with the backs of his fingers.

'I'm fine.' His voice rang in his ears like a child's, and he wished he hadn't spoken. There was a silence as he had difficulty believing that those eyes had been following him. 'Thank you.'

'Oh, not at all. I am just so glad to have been here for you. What if you had been alone? You know there are not too many people who come here at this time of night.' Her concern was almost too attractive for the world.

He couldn't think of a single contribution to this simple conversation.

'Why are you here?' she asked. She wasn't accusing him or prying. She was just asking.

He had not thought to prepare for this question. He couldn't reply honestly, so he lied. 'To dump some rubbish.'

'But you have not got any rubbish. I know you did yesterday because I looked at it, but you did not bring any with you tonight. I saw.' Her eyes narrowed and her head tilted. 'Why are you here?' This time she was prying a little, and it made her even lovelier.

He stood immobile, with a cut across his face and having just been caught lying. He wished he had never left his flat. In desperation he thrust his hands into his trouser pockets and fished around. He pulled out an old tram ticket, waved it in the air and threw it on to the ground.

'There.'

'Where have you come from?' she asked.

'Town.'

'All the way from town?'

'Yes.'

'At this time of night?'

'Yes.' His voice wobbled. He felt like a defendant whose case was crumbling around him at the appearance of some unexpected and irrefutable evidence.

'This is a long way to come at night.'

'Yes.' He wished he could think of something else to say, and that he had never been born.

'Still, at least you have the welkin's luminescence to light your way.'

'Yes. Yes, I do.'

'But to come all this way in the almost dark and to climb over the fence and to risk being caught and everything, and only for a tram ticket?' She looked directly at him as if the world was about to end, and it was somehow all her fault. 'Oh why are you here?'

He was desperate. His mind was a brilliant expanse of nothing. He looked around, looked ashamed and mumbled. 'Because I like rubbish.' The instant he said it he knew what a mess he had made. He had disgraced himself in front of her, and would never be able to face her, or even himself, again.

Suddenly she came to life, jumping up and down with a blinding smile across her face. It was the first time he had seen her looking anything other than mortified, and his stomach burned as though he had swallowed a hot coal.

'Oh, I am so glad,' she cried. 'I know it is hard to say it, but you are just like me. Oh, it is so hard to tell people for they think you to be idiotic or a bit funny or something when you tell them how you like rubbish. But no, you do not have to hide this from me. Now I understand why you are here. You feel for all of this.' She swept her arm around, indicating the whole site. 'Just like me.'

He smiled at the success of his lie. It was only small, so he didn't feel too guilty about it.

She dabbed his wound for the final time and turned to go.

Then she turned again and said, 'I think we two shall meet again. Goodbye.' She dashed away from him, her gauze and her hair waving behind her as she vanished into the mounds of black, white and grey.

Third

Everything became pointless that did not have something to do with her. She was the focus of his every thought. When he worked he worked for her, to buy her the things she needed and wanted. Every time he picked up his plane or his chisel, he knew that he had only ever learned to use them for her; to make money for her, and of course to make her anything her heart desired. When he thought, he thought only of his future with the girl, Maria. Her name had come back to him, and it filled his every moment. All his internal dialogue was now addressed to her, and her gentle voice filled his mind's ear. Her image perched parrot-like on his shoulder, and he wanted to run the tip of his nose along her soft brown back.

The third time they met she didn't stop for long. He was in a different part of the site from before, and had been frantically looking for her for three hours. She came into view, apparently in a hurry to go somewhere. Even so she stopped for a talk, despite looking devastated.

'Hello again,' she said. 'It is such a nice evening, do you not think?'

'Yes.' His tongue turned to pâté at the sight of her. Her hair was tied back from her face, and lay in a single plait down her back. He saw her little ears for the first time. They didn't carry any jewellery, and he thought the world of them. He struggled for something to say. She was wearing what looked like a car seat cover. It was furry and tiger skin, and allowed him to see her bare, smooth shoulders. Suddenly he wanted to fell an ancient oak and carve a statue of her. He looked at her feet, and at last thought of a question. 'How come you can run around the landfill site in your bare feet? Don't you get hurt?'

She looked puzzled, as though she had never considered this before. 'Well, I suppose my feet are so dainty that it does not matter. I . . .' She sank into sullen contemplation. 'I have very dainty feet.'

He looked at them. They were dainty. He had noticed this before. She carried on.

'Sometimes,' she sighed, 'with feet like mine, it is like walking on air.' What life there had been drained from her face, and she bowed her head. 'It is like being a little fairy.'

'Yes. It must be. It must be just like being a little fairy.'

'But I must go now. I hope you do not consider me rude, but we will meet again and talk about all of this.' Again she swept her arm around, indicating all the rubbish that surrounded them.

'Yes.'

She dashed away, her pristine feet barely touching the slime and shards beneath. From the distance she turned and called to him. 'Your face looks so much better.'

He watched her until she was out of sight, wondering how anybody could care as much as she cared.

The sun rose as he jumped down from the fence.

Fourteenth

Their meetings continued, but some nights he failed to find her. He had begun to worry that she realised why he was there. Often when they met she looked so sad, as if she were about to burst into tears, and would simply say 'Hello' or 'Oh' and pass on her way with a look of confusion. He wanted to talk to her about rubbish, because talking about it would bring them together, and maybe make her love him.

His love had convinced him that lurking among all this business was a real chance of a romantic union. Wild thoughts filled his mind. He began to wonder whether she had a lover. The image of her with someone else filled him with fury and sadness, and he tried as hard as he could to banish it. His longing for her to be inviolable was exceeded only by his desire to spend the rest of his life making love to her.

He decided that the time had come to make firmer advances towards her. One evening, when the moon was almost full and he could see her clearer than ever, he took a bottle of wine with him to the site. Despite looking full of cares, she was in a talkative mood and noticed it in his hand.

'You have brought a bottle to dump. Where are you going to leave it?'

'Well, I was going to drop it here, but I just realised I must have picked up the wrong bag on my way out. You see, the bottle's full, and there are two glasses and a corkscrew in this bag. I don't know how it could have happened.' Suddenly fear thrilled through his veins, and he became convinced that he would be a bad kisser.

'Oh, then you must carry everything back over the fence and all the way to your home again.'

'Yes, I suppose so. Unless . . .' She didn't respond to this pause, and he felt stupid as he carried on. 'Unless you would like to join me for a glass.'

'Oh, I do not know if I should drink wine with you. Maybe I would become drunk.'

'Just one glass won't make you drunk. You could tell me about the site, about your love of landfill. There's so much I want to know.' It was true. He wanted to know about this thing she loved so much, so they could love it together and have it in common.

'Oh, why not?' She broke into a reckless smile, her perfect teeth sparkling more brilliantly than the stars.

They sat side by side on a rusting, overturned refrigerator. He opened the bottle, poured a glass for Maria and handed it to her, trying not to shake. He poured one for himself and they drank, at Maria's suggestion, to a range of solutions to one of man's oldest problems: the disposal of waste.

He relaxed for the first time since they had met. Having her by his side seemed normal and right. 'Tell me about dumps, Maria. Tell me about all this.'

'Oh, where to start?' Suddenly the sad expression he had so often seen reappeared. 'Where to start?'

'What was it that first attracted you to landfill?' He had been rehearsing this question for days, and was pleased with the way he said it.

'Well it is just like ants, do you not think? It is like beautiful rivers of ants,' she began, sipping as he watched her lips and wanted to kiss them. 'I remember when I was four and I asked my mother where all the rubbish went and she said, "To the tip, Maria," and I wondered what the tip looked like and then I went up in a balloon about one year later.'

'A balloon?'

'Yes, it was my birthday when I was five and my mother and father loved me so much that they took me up in a balloon, up into the sky over our village. They kept telling me to look at this and that. "Look at the cows, Maria," "Look at the smoke puffing out of all the chimneys, Maria," "Look at the beautiful fields and rivers, Maria." Oh, they loved me so much. And I looked at these things and I liked them, but the thing I looked at most of all was a little dustcart. I saw it pick up bins from outside all the houses, and the rubbish went in the back of it. Then the wind started to blow us towards the tip and the balloon man was sad because he thought I would not like to see the tip from the sky, but I said I was glad and before long we were flying right over it. I could see it quite clearly from the air, and it was all just like ants. The little ants in the village making their piles of rubbish, the little ants with the dustcart picking it up, and the little ants on the landfill site, going around and doing their little jobs. I waved at the tip men, and some of them waved back at me. Everything I saw from the sky had something to do with rubbish. The site was like a magnificent firth, and all of the people on the ground were streams running towards it, little knowing of the incredible process of which they were all a part. You see, the people were making or growing things, then other people were buying those things, then they were becoming, in part, rubbish, then the people were throwing the rubbish out, the rubbish was going to the tip in a special truck and was being left there, and before too long there would be more to be discarded and so on and so forth. Oh, it is just like the emmets as they go along the ground. I make it sound so simple, but it is really not simple at all. Then, when the balloon had landed in a field, all the way back to my house I looked for dustcarts and dustbins and oh, it was so nice to have seen it all from the sky. It was just too beautiful, and ever since that day I have spent my life studying and loving all of this.' She swept her arm around. 'Landfill.'

'And it all ends here,' he said. 'With this mess.' He looked at the rubbish then looked at her, so small and wonderful. He wondered how anyone this perfect could be so interested in waste.

'No.' She clenched her fists, and her voice filled with passion. 'No, that is what everyone says but it does not finish like this. Not at all. I think it is strange that people know and care so little for something that is such a central part of their lives. Of course this is not the end, not even in this throwaway society.'

'What do you mean? Surely the rubbish is dumped here, and that's the end of it?'

'No. That is not it at all. Do you know nothing of landfill?'

He felt ashamed. 'No, not really,' he admitted. 'I only know I like it.'

'Oh. I thought you knew some things about it.' He couldn't tell whether she was angry or not.

'No. I don't. I'm just starting to learn.' He looked at her eyes, and smiled. 'Maybe you could teach me.'

She didn't look back, and he felt like a grinning fool.

'Oh, then you must listen to me,' she continued. 'This is not the end of the waste. No, not in a competently managed site. You see, landfill is a long-term proposition, more so than you realise. As we scar the earth with quarries and open mines, it is also our responsibility to make it well again. People do not appreciate that landfill can do this, and that it is not just a big, nasty field of litter. Just as a scab covers a wound until the time is right for it to fall off and reveal the healed skin beneath, so does the landfill site pass into a new incarnation. If you think this will be an expanse of rubbish in fifty years, then you are mistaken.'

'What will it be like, then?' He wanted to learn, and her to rest her little head on his shoulder.

'If I have anything to do with the site's policy development it will be a beautiful park and nature reserve. It will take patience and vision, but under the right management it will happen.'

'But how?'

'Well, when the site is full, it will be landscaped and planted and designed to be a beautiful asset to the area. People are so short-sighted, and they fail to see the potential for true beauty in competently managed waste disposal.'

He felt this was aimed at him. As she sipped her wine he winced a little and felt stupid.

'Look at my arm,' she commanded. 'Is there anything wrong with it?'

He looked at it as closely as the moon and stars would allow. It was slender, brown and coated with an almost imperceptible down. It was perfect.

'No.'

'Of course there is nothing wrong with it, but can you believe that less than one year ago I was injured in a frightful accident, and blood was pouring from a long, deep gash just here?' She traced a line along her forearm.

The thought of her in pain made him angry. He wished he

had been there for her, to support her through such a terrible time.

'Of course you can believe it,' she told him. 'Look at your face, where it was bleeding that time when you fell over. Yes, there is a thin pink line now, but soon there will be no trace of anything dreadful ever having happened to you. It will have healed, and so it is with landfill. Do you have a pen?' she asked.

'Yes.' He always carried a pen and a piece of paper in case she wanted to write anything about herself, or if she asked for his address or something.

'Then look,' and she spent the next few minutes drawing very, very seriously.

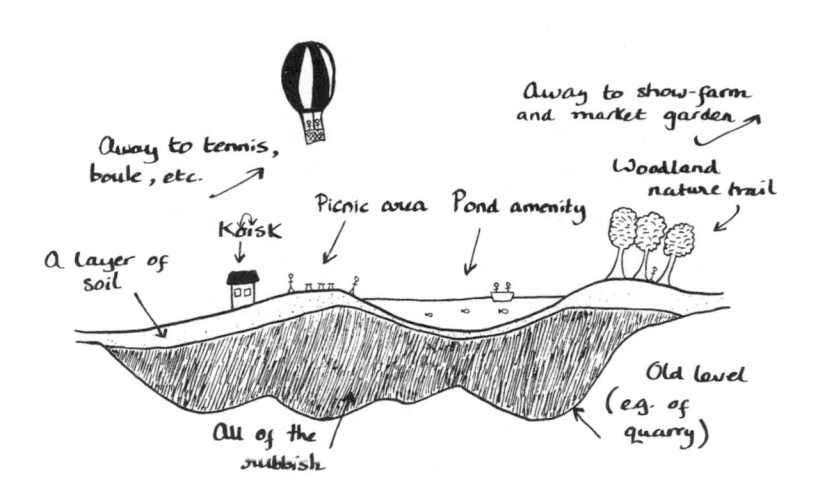

'So, you can see. From a void created by the extraction of sand, gravel or hoggin, to all of this waste around us,' she swept her arm around, 'and then to this,' and she waved the picture under his nose, looking almost too sad for him to bear. 'It will even pay for its own upkeep with revenue from the market garden and leisure facilities. It will cost the community nothing, and should even make a profit. The people of the area can only benefit.'

'I see now,' he said, wishing to appear a keen student. 'All this will be attractive parkland as well as being agriculturally productive. It'll be a beautiful asset to the area, and before long people will barely remember that below the ground lies all this waste.'

'Exactly. It will be a very good amenity, do you not think?'

'Yes,' he said. 'Very good. Excellent, even.' There was a silence. To fill it he asked, 'But will it really happen?' Despite the slight air of friction, he could feel them getting closer. Becoming friends.

'Of course it will happen, given forward-thinking management. Why would it not?'

'Well, maybe there would be dangers.'

'Dangers? No. There would be no dangers. None at all. I do not understand you.'

'But how about this?' He took the pen from her hand. It was warm. He turned the paper over and drew.

'So,' he said, 'there you have all the pretty parkland, but underneath there's a hole left by the decomposition of a cluster of compostible matter. It undermines the strength of the surface and one day, maybe in a hundred years, this happens.' He picked a piece of cardboard from the ground and drew again.

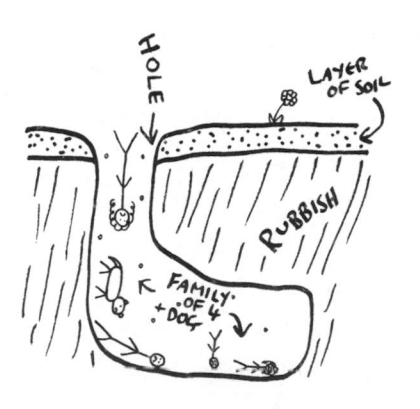

'Subsidence. Surely it's a danger.'

She snatched the cardboard from his hand, threw it to one side and said, 'No. You have so much to learn.'

'I know,' he conceded. The last thing he wanted was to get into an argument with her.

'I am speaking only of well managed sites. If you wish we can sit here all night and talk of badly run places, but that is a different topic altogether, and one in which I have scant interest. But really, I must not keep you. You are very busy. You have so much to do, so much to learn. Thank you so much for the glass of wine. I am not at all dizzy. Goodnight.' She went away.

He walked home, wondering how well the evening had gone.

Twentieth

He knew so little about her, and all of it was good. She was beautiful, she was caring, she was intelligent, she was everything. But still he knew so little about her. He filled the gaps in his knowledge with imaginings and assumptions, all of them as attractive as the fragments he knew. He could see no way that she could ever fail to live up to his perception of her, and was able to feel that he loved her absolutely. He did love her absolutely. He even loved her perpetual sadness. He saw it as the focus for his contribution to their romance. By loving her, he would make her happy.

He made her a mug tree. He spent hours on it, staying behind after work to make it strong and to engrave it with patterns designed specially for her. He put all his love into it, and took it to the landfill site twice before finding the courage to present it to her.

'I've got something for you,' he said, reaching into his plastic bag.

'Oh?'

'Yes. Here.' He pulled out the mug tree and handed it to her, hoping she hadn't noticed him shaking.

'Oh.'

'Do you like it?'

She seemed so sad that he had given her this gift. 'Oh, I

think you are very funny.' She smiled uncomfortably for a second, before returning to her usual expression.

'You don't like it?' She didn't seem to.

'Oh, it is very funny of you. You know, my lover gave me one of these things, but he was very serious.'

He went cold and looked away. He wanted to kick someone. He wanted to smash someone's face. He wanted to cry. But he knew he couldn't do any of these, so he simply sat in silence as his heart struggled to escape from his body.

'Yes, my lover came to my window one night.'

He didn't want to hear this, but felt compelled to sit and listen as though they were having just another conversation about the brightness of the stars.

'He called out for me, and climbed up and gave me one of these things. I do not know why. I think he thought that I would want it or something. You know he even made it especially for me and it took him days to do. I told him that I liked it, and we made love until the morning.'

He was able to wipe a tear from his eye as if it were an itch. She didn't notice, and carried on.

'But you are so funny to bring one to me. I think you picked it up from the tip, because they are everywhere. Every day I see them. You have a funny way with your jokes.'

He desperately tried not to think of the love he had put into the mug tree, but he wanted to stop her as her arm came back and she threw it as far as she could. She was strong, and it landed next to skeletal remains of a chest of drawers a long way away. He saw one of its arms snap off.

She carried on. 'Oh, my lover, he loved me more than anything. But no, we were not meant to be together and this mug tree showed that. How could I love someone who thinks of me so wrongly? One who thinks that I want a nice kitchen and a nice mug tree to go in it? No, the gift was a part of his dream, not mine. It was a gift to himself, I think. Even though we made love until the dawn, when we had finished I told him to go and I never saw him again. I never saw him, only the flowers he sent and the letters he wrote, pleading for me to accept him back because he loved me so much. As far as I know he still loves me and he always will.' She hung her head.

As this lover drifted into the past tense he felt a little better. But he was still shocked and saddened to find that she had known a man, and had allowed him so close to her. As he walked home, he had no idea what to think about anything. He had worked hard to expel from his thoughts the image of her with a lover, but now he could see nothing but her tongue flicking in and out of someone else's mouth. He had wanted to be the first and last man she ever kissed. Only one thing was certain as he lay awake that night: that he didn't love her any less for what she had done. He didn't know why, but if anything he loved her even more.

The memory of her throwing the mug tree away made his tear ducts open so wide that he wondered where all the salt water could be coming from. He imagined a reservoir swilling around behind his eyes. On its surface walked Maria, her little feet bone-dry.

He had not pictured her in a kitchen with her mug tree; he had just thought that she would like a nice present. When he woke up he felt as if someone had been beating him around the head all night.

Twenty-sixth

His gift had made her smile, if only for a second and for all the wrong reasons. He decided to play the fool for her. Sometimes as she dashed past he would pick up a piece of rubbish, whatever came to hand, and offer it to her or put it on his head. She rarely smiled for longer than a moment. Usually she just said hello, and continued on her way, leaving him feeling ludicrous. There were some dreadful, endless evenings when he didn't see her at all.

The twenty-sixth time they met, she looked more beautiful than he had ever seen her. She was wearing a wide-brimmed hat, a black fur coat that almost touched the ground and, for the first time, shoes. They were black too, and had very high heels. Her hair was brushed and silky, and carried perfect reflections of the moon and stars. He wanted to tell her how beautiful she was looking. She was beautiful, but she was also sadder than he had ever seen her. Her eyes were red, and she sniffed. She had obviously been crying.

'I like your outfit,' he said.

'Oh, thank you,' she whispered, her voice cracking with emotion. 'It is so nice, and to think I found it here on this landfill site. The coat, the hat and the shoes. They suit me so well. They make me look so nice, so pretty. So much so that I think perhaps I should never have worn them.'

'Is this a special occasion?' he asked, and as he did he was struck by the appalling realisation that she could be dressed up to meet someone else.

'Yes. Well, it was but it is no longer. Now it is such a sad day.' She started to cry, and he wanted to kiss her sorrow away. Instead he stood still, not knowing what to do.

'I am sorry,' she sobbed, dabbing her eyes with her fur. 'Do not worry. I will be all right.'

'What is it?' he asked. 'What's wrong?'

They sat together on a different fridge.

'Oh, today has been too terrible.'

'But why?'

'Because ever since I was a little girl of five and I went up in the balloon, all I have wanted to do was to work in waste disposal, and one day to manage a landfill site and to oversee it as it turns from a bare expanse into a big tip, and then into a beautiful, lovely place for people to go to. And today, for one more time, I was told that I could not. For one year I have been applying to be a junior manager for sites such as this, travelling from one to the next. And every time it is the same, just like today. It is really just so sad, and I think I must give up.'

'What happened?'

'Well, I met the boss of here, of this place, and had an interview with him and some others and they asked me some questions which I answered very well, and they told me I could not have a job here after all.'

'Why not?'

'For many reasons. It seems that everything is wrong about me. It is always the same. They do not believe that I am serious. They say to me, "Oh, Maria, you are only seventeen years old and maybe you are a fickle, flighty thing and will change your mind about working here. You are just a young woman and surely you will want to explore, to have adventures and fun. You must not tie yourself to such a demanding job as this." Oh, why do they not understand? They think my love of landfill is nothing more than a silly phase for a silly girl. They do not know that this is all I will ever want.'

'But maybe if you try again in a few years' time you'll get the job. Don't lose hope, Maria.' His arm twitched, waiting for the right moment to draw her towards his supportive, reassuring shoulder.

'Oh no, because there is always one other reason. They say, "But Maria, you are so beautiful. We have never seen anyone quite like you, and we cannot imagine you lasting in this business. Soon you will meet a handsome, strong man and he will become your lover and then your husband and you will be very happy and thoughts of waste disposal will become overshadowed by dreams of your home and your lovely little children." I am such a sweet flower, you know. I always have been and I suppose I will be forever. Even when I was a little girl people saw my beauty and fled from it. They have always, always thought that because I am so small and so beautiful to look at, I could not want to know them or listen to what they are saying. So they run from me. It is just so sad for me.' Again she cried, and wiped her tears with the tips of her fingers.

He tried some words of encouragement. 'But maybe this isn't the site for you, Maria. Maybe you should look for one that you can start from scratch. Here you'd be taking over a site that's already full.' He was ready to follow her throughout the world. He didn't care where he was, as long as she was there too.

'Hardly,' she spluttered. 'This site has not yet reached fifteen percent of its capacity. From a regenerative perspective, it is more or less a blank canvas.' She flew into sobs, groans and tears.

Eventually she was able to carry on. 'It all seems too unfair. My knowledge of the administrative and legislative framework for waste management belies my seventeen years. If only they would give me a chance to demonstrate my expertise, commitment and ability.'

He didn't know what to do or say. His arm continued to shake, but she was right. She was too beautiful to be comforted.

'And,' she choked, 'it is so hard for me to find a friend through all of this. People are scared of me, scared of my beauty, or else they are jealous of it. All my lovers have loved me so much that I have never been able to find out who they really are. My looks fill them with wonder, all of them, and they change in front of me. They act stupidly and differently. Women are too envious of my long shiny hair, my supple shape and my exquisite features to speak to me, and all men act the fool in front of me. All of them. Like you, with your silly jokes. You do this just to impress me because you have never known anyone as beautiful as I am, and you do not know how to behave when I am near you. You are in love with me, I know it. You are just like all of the others, I can tell. Because I have the fairest fleece of all the flock they adore me and are stupid for me, or they hate me because they know they will never have me to themselves. It is always one or the other, and it is no different with you. It is no different at all.'

He looked at her. She was looking away. She had known of his love from the start.

'I think you have little interest in rubbish. I used to hope that maybe, just maybe, you meant what you said, and that we would become best friends. But no. You simply want to be close to me, to kiss my pretty lips and to be loved by me forever. That is all.'

Since the first time they met he had wondered how she would react to the inevitable revelation of his love. He had imagined her falling into his arms, slapping his face or crying with confusion or pity; anything but sighing wearily and looking away.

'I'm sorry,' he said. 'I'm really, really sorry.' He meant it too. He was sad, sorry and ashamed.

'It is all right. I understand. It is something to which I have become used. Goodbye.' He watched as she slowly walked away, hunched slightly and reaching up to wipe the occasional tear from her face.

Then she turned and walked back towards him. He was still sitting on the fridge. As she came closer he wondered when she was going to stop. She only did when she reached him and her tongue was in his mouth and her fingers playing roughly with his hair. Even then she pressed so hard against him that he thought she was trying to force her way through his body and out the other side.

When she finally pulled back, her coat fell open and her breasts hung before him, looking even more perfect than he had ever imagined. As he stroked and squeezed them he felt so bewildered that he could almost have run away. He tried to gaze romantically into her eyes, but her head was always turned away, or her eyes shut tight. She pulled him around as if he were a rag doll, shifting him into position. Without knowing how it had happened he found himself inside her. He felt her warmth and kissed her face as she slipped up and down, breathing deeply, growling slightly, and scratching his skin with her long nails. Her thighs were the softest things he had ever felt. As he kissed her neck and played with her right nipple, her head flew back, her hat fell off and she howled. It was over for both of them, and with a last gentle, lingering kiss she dismounted, pulled his clothes back into place and, without once letting him see her eyes, picked up her hat and vanished into the rubbish. As the final strands of her hair slipped from his fingers, his look of disbelief changed into a smile that didn't leave his face until he was back in his flat and drifting off to sleep with her scent clinging to his skin.

Twenty-seventh and final

The following evening he took an enormous bunch of red roses to the site. He searched everywhere until he found her, looking unbelievable in baggy blue trousers and a man's shirt on top of a mound of newly delivered industrial waste. Her sleeves were rolled up, and she smiled and waved when she saw him. He had never seen her so happy. He wanted to dance with her.

'Hello Maria,' he said. 'I've brought these for you.' She fluttered down from her hillock, took the flowers, sniffed them and hugged them tightly to her chest.

'Oh, thank you so much. They are so pretty. Almost as pretty as me.' She sniffed them again and smiled at him. Everything felt right.

'This is such a special day for me,' she said. 'I am so happy. It is not at all like yesterday. Yesterday I was so sad. You saw me, I was crying. Do you remember?'

'Of course I remember. What's happened to cheer you up?' he asked, knowing she was about to say that her happiness was all because of their love for one another, and that they must kiss and be together forever.

'Because I went to see the boss of here again and I implored, I fell at his feet, and I lay before him in a heap, saying, "Oh please sir, oh give me a chance to prove my commitment, my dedication to this site. Oh please." I outlined my philosophy and my ideas for updating the council's waste disposal programme, and for catapulting this site into the global vanguard of landfill, where ecological sensitivity and public support meet developmental progress and cost-efficiency.'

'What did he say?'

'He looked at me, and he said, "Maria, I will tell you this. I have been wondering how one as perfect, small and special as you could ever dedicate herself to a career in this mucky business. To be honest I still have my doubts, but you have convinced me that you have a genuine interest in the field. I am willing to give you a try." That is what the boss of here said to me.'

'So he gave you the job? Are you a junior manager of this place?'

'Well no. No, not yet. He said, "Maria, I will give you a short contract, for just a few months, to drive a bulldozer. If that goes well, I will change your role to an administrative one, and if after a year I feel you have proved your commitment to working here I will place you on an initial management training programme. Maria," he said, "you start work tomorrow." He said that to me. So maybe one day I will rise to be the boss of all this.' She swept her arm around.

'Congratulations,' he said. 'So you'll be staying around here.'

'Yes, I will be living in a caravan on the site, somewhere far over there.' She pointed. 'But I will no longer be able to roam as freely as I do today. My new boss says that I have only been allowed to stay here living as I have because I am so beautiful. Otherwise I would have been evicted a long time ago. But it is not sad for me because I will like my caravan and it will be a nice house to live in, I think. Maybe I will even have a mug tree.' Her smile put the moon to shame. 'So from now I must behave and be responsible and work so very hard, and I think I must even wear some proper clothes.'

'I hope I'll still be able to climb in here.'

'Oh no,' she smiled. 'They have already listened to my idea to put an electric fence around the site, one you cannot see through, and it will go up in a day or two. I want no one to come in here until the great day when the fence comes down and all this is hectare upon hectare of beauty, for as far as the eye can see.' She swept her arm around. 'Oh, I am so happy.'

He smiled, as if he too were happy at this. 'Oh, then I'll visit you at your caravan.'

She looked away as the joy fell from her face and her old expression returned. 'Oh no,' she muttered, looking uneasily at an upturned pram. 'I think they do not allow visitors. It is a security measure.'

'But if they don't allow visitors, how will we meet?'

'I do not know. I had not really thought about it.'

'We'll have to think of a way.'

'Why?'

The question nearly knocked him over. 'Because I love you, Maria. You know that. I have to see you.'

She looked into the night. 'This is very awkward for me.'

'You know how I feel about you, Maria. How can we not see each other after everything that's happened?'

'I do not know what to say to you.' She thought for a while. 'Listen to me please. You have no chance with me.'

'What? But you must at least let me try, Maria. Would you object if I were to pursue you?'

'Yes. Yes, I would. I am not at all interested, and that is that.'

'But I love you, Maria.' He tried not to cry. There was a very long silence. 'Look, even if I don't chase you, can we be friends?'

'Of course we can be friends. That is not a problem for us. Friendship never ends.'

'Good.' There was a catch in his voice. 'That's something.'

'I must go now. Thank you so much for all the pretty flowers.' She sniffed them, and smiled again. 'Oh, I am so happy. Tomorrow I drive my bulldozer for the very first time. Goodbye, and I am so sorry for you.' Her lips brushed his cheek with a farewell kiss, and she turned to go.

'Wait,' he cried. 'When will I see you again?'

'Oh, I do not know. Whenever, I suppose.'

'Shall I come here, or should we meet somewhere else?'

She paused. 'Maybe it would be best if we did not meet at all.'

'But you said we were friends. How can we be friends if we never meet?'

'Oh, it is easy,' she said, and disappeared.

Afterwards

Her absence from his life didn't make him think of her or love her any less. She still filled his every moment. He constantly spoke to her in his mind, made little things for her, hatched plans for the two of them and dreamed of what she could be doing at that moment. Knowing that she was living her life, being happy and getting along without him was too upsetting to bear. He tried hard not to think about it, but there were times when he could not help it. They would never be together. He would never hold her hand as they walked along the street, or make bunk-beds for their little boys and girls. When these thoughts appeared he wanted to die.

Sometimes the conversations he and Maria were holding in his head would begin to sound hollow. So instead of just thinking them, he said them. He would speak aloud under his breath, and Maria's sweet voice would chime her loving reply in his mind. Sometimes the truth crept up on him unexpectedly, and his sudden bursts of muttered one-sided dialogue lost him his job. No one would speak to him any more.

'Don't worry,' he would say in the street or the butcher's, or anywhere. 'I'll have those shelves up by tomorrow.'

'She's looking poorly. Do you think she should have the day off school?'

...o look beautiful today. As always.' As always. You've got such a [...]tty smile [...] knew that would make you smile.

People pitied and avoided him. As the truth became more insistent his voice grew louder. Whenever reality tried to force its way into his life, he tried as hard as he could to drown it out. His speech turned from a mumble into a shout. 'Yes, I think so too,' he would suddenly cry in the street, in agreement with whatever it was his Maria had just said.

He sent a letter to her at the landfill site, wishing her well in her new job and her new home. He didn't mention his love for her, or the night they were together, but said that it would be nice to see her again soon. He could have written anything, because it was returned unopened. She must have known it was from him and arranged for it to be sent back so he was not afflicted by false hope. That was so kind of her, and made him love her all the more. He

As she lived her new life behind the live wire, he thought of ways of contacting her and of winning her love. This was also carved and sent a fruit bowl for her caravan. He became desperate to communicate with her.

One evening before bin day he crept into the dark as he had done so many times before. This time, though, he didn't go to the tip. He had carved a simple message, 'I LOVE

---

and every day, even on weekends, she [...] of the site in her hard hat and her little [...] rything and making plans. She was so

[...]him sadder and sadder, and by this [...]perpetual imaginary conversations [...]ve didn't wane for a second. His [...]his every action.

[...]hat public confidence in every [...]nt process is the key to a [...]hat the local people's lives [...]olicy developments. The [...]nd the beautiful, clever [...]the site that she never [...]es loved her because [...]ation programmes [...]cipal lighting and [...]up, thereby extending its [...]nancial viability and safeguarding [...]obs. A small composting programme pro-[...]hough methane to heat all the town's public [...]uildings, and cylinders of gas were offered to council employees as incentives for hard work. Rates went down, the town began to prosper, and the future for coming generations was bright, as employment from the impending market garden or from general maintenance work at the landscaped leisure area was more or less guaranteed for all those who wanted it. Lorry movements through residential areas were curtailed by a series of sensitive diversions, and her commercial and statutory waste minimisation initiative was popular with the council and the community, and surprised everyone except its initiator with its profitability.

The tip workers were also very fond of their new boss. One day, as he was dropping an elaborate but durable toast rack into a bin, he heard one of them boasting to a friend about spending a whole lunch hour in her caravan, making love to her. This man spoke of her exceptionally long hair, her pretty face and her lovely shape that yielded so expertly to his demands. The man's offer to leave his wife for her had been turned down. '"You know, I have many lovers,"' the man said, crudely imitating Maria's precious voice, '"so I will not marry you. But you are handsome and I like you and you give me much pleasure, so we will make love again before too long. Do not worry. Now get back to work."'

From that moment he cried all the time, just little tears that could not be seen from a distance and low, quiet sobs that sounded almost like hiccups. Even when he didn't have a gift ready for her he would go through people's rubbish, gently touching it. He knew that her little feet would soon be dancing across it. He tried to touch as much waste as he could. As he went from bin to bin, he imagined his tears and the touch of his hands making his presence take root over

...would sto... ...bowl, clmb down ...n, know who it ws from, ...y spent together, smile and realise ...ove with him after all. ...arted to do more and more things like this. He spent ...us days making love tokens and dropping them in bins. He became so absorbed in his efforts to win Maria that he no longer thought to wash or shave. He became less furtive about everything, and walked around during the daylight hours dropping little wooden things into dustbins. Salad servers, necklaces with 'MARIA', carved into each tiny bead, or sturdy little boxes for her to store all the trinkets that he gave her. They were all made carefully, lovingly and perfectly.

Sometimes he overheard pieces of news about her. Three years after the last time he saw her, he heard somebody say that there was a new deputy manager at the tip, and that she was only twenty and apparently very little and extremely pretty. Not long afterwards, he heard somebody say that someone old had retired, and the beautiful girl had been appointed overall manager of the site and was doing a very good job there. Her ideas were benefiting homes and the whole site. He wanted her more than ever, and was prepared to forget the stories he had heard about her lovers, and continue their romance where it had ended on that perfect night.

One afternoon, many years after the last time he had seen Maria, when rumours had filtered into the community that she was already beginning to plant trees and sculpt ponds on certain areas of the site, he lifted the lid off a bin as usual. Crying, and speaking aloud to the woman he adored, the emaciated, dirty, straggle-bearded man took from his pocket a little wooden heart. He had spent days making it for her. It was designed to be exactly the same size as the palm of her hand, and there was an inscription on it. Its tiny writing read, 'I still love you Maria. If you ever need me for anything I will always be here for you. I hope you are happy, because nothing else matters to me. Nothing.'

As he carefully placed it in the bin a woman passed him, holding on to her little daughter's hand. 'What's that funny man doing?' asked the girl.

The mother cast him an uneasy, embarrassed glance. The weeping, muttering man she had seen so many times before had clearly heard.

'Nothing,' she said, pulling her daughter along as fast as she could without it seeming obvious that she wanted to get her away from him as quickly as possible. 'Nothing. He's just looking for something.'

The girl needed to know more. 'What? What's he looking for?'

'Just something he's lost, I expect. He's just looking for something he's thrown away by mistake.'

The Painting

In his small clearing deep in the woods, The Artist stood alone before his easel. He took his finest brush, carefully dipped it in the last of his white paint and very slowly raised it to the canvas. With intense concentration he applied the tiniest speck of light to her left eye, giving it the living sparkle it had lacked. After weeks of indecisions and revisions, he had finished. He stood back to look at his work.

She was perfect. Her long, pink legs seemed soft enough to dive into, and her hair covered all things immodest with its golden waves without detracting at all from the evident glory beyond. Her figure was neither skinny nor plump but just right, and the long, slender fingers that played with her tresses were so real that he felt he could hold them and gently kiss them one by one. Her face was the prettiest he had ever seen. It was not classically structured; it was just really, really pretty. Her blue eyes smiled at him, her lips were slightly open, seeming to invite his to land on them, and her cheeks blushed a little at the depth of his scrutiny. As he had been painting her, he had decided that she had just that moment blossomed from a pretty girl into an incredible woman, a little shy of the attention her beauty was receiving, but glad of it and, in her innocence, wondering how to respond to all the new feelings coursing through her body.

Naturally he fell in love with her.

All he could do was look at her. As the sun set and his legs became weary, he sat on the ground without taking his eyes off her. When night came he quickly lit a fire a safe distance away, and even though she was indistinct he looked at her without relief until dawn came and her beauty was once again lit by the sun. He did not notice the earwigs and the millipedes crawling over him, nor the line of ants that marched across his legs. He did not really notice anything but the pretty girl. He did not notice his body pleading for sleep, food and water. Instead he looked at the bare shoulder he had painted peeping through her hair, and fell more in love as each moment passed.

It took only three days for his body to fail. He died cross-legged with his eyes open, looking until the last at the girl he loved.

A little more than a week later, three men from the village were led to the scene by their dogs, who had caught and pursued the unusual scent of the body. As they beat their way through the undergrowth and entered the clearing, they noticed not what little was left of The Artist, but the glorious picture of the girl. One of them gave a quiet sigh, which the others did not seem to hear; they just approached the painting, stepping over The Artist's body to get the best view they could.

They had never seen anyone as perfect as her before. She did not seem unreal or untouchable. No, there was something natural and accessible about her. Two of the men had attractive wives, the other a small, delicately featured lover whom he planned to marry. But now, with this girl so close, the women they had loved so much for so long seemed ordinary. The longing they had always felt while on hunting trips ebbed with every moment spent looking at the painting. As they grew tired they tried hard to keep their eyes open, for every blink was a moment away from her.

At the time when they would usually have been packing away their boules or their dominoes, heading excitedly up the ladders of their small wooden homes and falling into the waiting arms of the women they loved, kissing their soft bodies and warm, damp mouths, and feeling the gentle brush of hair on their skin, the sun disappeared.

The pain they felt while scrabbling in the dark for wood was tempered only by the knowledge that very soon the fire would be alight and they would be able to see the painting again.

By the time the dogs accompanying the search party found the clearing, two of the men had died and the one who was still clinging to life was propped upright against his friends' bodies; his eyes mere slits but open just wide enough to see the picture of the girl. The fire smouldered nearby.

All the men from the village had joined the hunt for their neighbours. As they crashed through the undergrowth they hardly paid any attention to the men for whom they had been searching so frantically, so taken were they by the lovely face, hair and figure of the girl in the painting. They sat around the easel in a tightly packed crescent, looking up at her and silently falling hopelessly, achingly in love.

They had a small amount of food and water within reach, and it was a few days before they started to die, their bodies slumping unnoticed where they sat and slowly being eaten by the small creatures of the forest.

The women from the village missed the men beyond belief as the days passed without their return. Their beds were cold and empty, and they longed to have their men back beside them. They wanted to kiss them until their lips were sore. Overcome with concern for their husbands and lovers, their sons and their brothers, they went together into the forest, hoping to find signs of them. They took with them skins full of water and bundles of little green apples. Once again it was dogs who guided them through the trees to the clearing.

Some of the men were clinging to life, their love for the girl keeping them going despite the lack of food and water. Others, recently dead, lay twisted, pale and ignored on the ground. Still others were unrecognisable, being in various states of decay, from grub-infested heaps of flesh to scavenged piles of bones.

The women could not believe what they saw. She was so pretty. Her hair was long, and shone like a field of corn on a perfect day, her figure was just right and her face was so lovely; it was knowing, innocent, alluring and demure all at once. They looked as hard as they could for little flaws, but could not find a single one. Silently they told themselves that she was not real, that she was just a painting and that they should not worry about her, but however hard they tried they began to feel awkward and unattractive next to her. They were too heavy or too thin; their hair too short or too straight; their faces bloated, or pinched and mean. They stood at the edge of the clearing, unnoticed by the dying men, who looked with failing eyes at the girl they loved.

Without saying a word the women headed back to the village, wishing their hands were not so worn, their breasts so low, and their hair so dull and lifeless.

Beautiful Consuela

Feliz

For as long as he could remember, everyone had expected Perico to marry a daughter of one of the many wealthy families of his father's acquaintance. Even he had expected this, and he had no objection. From childhood he had been introduced to strings of these girls, and had grown fond of many of them. Without exception, they adored him. He was tall, athletic, wonderful company and outstandingly handsome, and his family had risen to become the wealthiest in the area. His only problem lay in choosing which girl to marry. His father's fellow merchants never seemed to tire of telling him that one day this girl or that girl, usually a daughter or a niece of theirs, would make someone a very happy husband. They would follow this with a wink, and the kind of smile usually seen only between scheming picaros.

To the perpetual impatience of his family he wavered

daily, sometimes even hourly, from one girl to another. He wanted to make sure that his future wife would be perfect.

Eventually he narrowed it down to two serious contenders: Inez and Juanita. Perico assured his parents that he would decide as quickly as possible which was to be his bride, so the father could be formally approached, and wedding plans made.

So it was almost as much of a surprise to him as it was to everyone else when he burst dishevelled into the dining hall and announced that he was going to marry a destitute farmer's beautiful daughter, whom he had met only that morning as she drove her decrepit mule through the woods.

Earlier that day he had gone riding in the woods on the pretext of hunting, but really to decide which of the two pretty girls, Inez or Juanita, he would most like to have as his own.

He felt ready to make his choice when something happened to disrupt his train of thought. His already light heart turned into a feather and floated away on the breeze. From around a bend a girl had appeared, driving a wood-laden mule. She had flowers in her long brown hair, and was wearing the same simple light brown dress that all the farm girls wore, its hem darkened by the dew. He thought that even the prettiest princess in all her robes and jewels could never even begin to approach the beauty of this girl. He felt sick, weak and powerless, and wondered if he would ever be able to do anything again.

The girl smiled at this stranger on horseback. She was surprised when he doffed his hat and offered to assist in any way he could. He was surprised to find he could still speak.

'Thank you for the offer,' she replied, 'but I make this walk several times a day. I'm sure I'll be fine on my own.'

'Then perhaps I could ride alongside you for company.' Immediately he regretted saying this, because she would probably say no.

She studied this handsome stranger for a moment. 'Fine.'

Perico turned his horse around. As he did, he saw her from behind. She had tucked her hair behind her left ear, and he noticed how small it was and how lovely, and how smooth her neck was, and how her dress revealed the perfect shape of her body. He caught up with her.

'Is this your mule?' he asked.

'Well, he's my father's.'

'How old is he?'

'He's about as old as me.'

He guessed him to be around sixteen or seventeen; just a few years younger than he was, anyway.

'I don't know how much longer the dear old thing will be able to carry firewood for us. He looks so weary.'

'Is your father a farmer?'

155

'Yes.'

'Do you have any brothers or sisters?'

'No, there's only me. My mother died when I was born.'

'You must be very precious to your father, then.'

'Yes. He's getting old.'

'Do you live near here?'

'Yes, just down there in fact, so goodbye. Maybe I'll see you again one day.' She headed down a small path just big enough for the old mule and his burden. He watched them disappear.

The moment she slipped out of sight he realised that he would not be able to live without seeing her fair skin again, or her long brown hair shining as it tumbled down her back.

'Wait,' he cried, and for a moment nothing happened. Then she reappeared, looking every bit as lovely as he had remembered.

'What is it?

He didn't know. 'It's a beautiful day.'

'Yes.' She looked puzzled.

'Look at the sky.' She did. It was blue. 'Could I talk to you for a while?'

'If you like.' Her smile showed her brilliant white teeth, gave her dimples and terrified Perico almost to death. She looked straight into his eyes. They tied their animals to trees and sat together on a grass bank. A black, red and bright yellow butterfly the size of a swallow fluttered by.

'Oh,' sighed the girl, delighted at this sight. 'You know, I've lived here all my life, among the birds and the butterflies and the fireflies and the flowers, but I never grow tired of them, and I don't suppose I ever will. Last night I spent an hour looking at an owl I had seen a hundred times before. It was just so lovely.'

Perico knew exactly what she meant. There are some things, though not many, so beautiful that they will never pall.

The girl knew the name of every creature that flew by. They heard the whisper of the breeze through the leaves, and looked at the flowers growing just about everywhere. She sat with her knees tucked up and her arms around them, hugging her skirt into the shape of her legs. Occasionally she would reach out and pick a flower, then weave it into her brown curls. She hummed a lovely tune which he had never heard before.

'What's that tune?' he asked her.

'I don't know.' She had no idea she had been humming.

She carried on, and as he listened he noticed a ladybird crawling into one of her beautiful curls. He reached over to coax it out.

'Ladybird,' he explained, as she stopped humming and looked quizzically at his big, clean, looming hand.

'Oh, I see,' she said, and without thinking reached up to help him. Their hands met. They both froze, each looking worriedly at the other for a moment, then they smiled. He put his arm around her, ran his hand up and down her back, and drew her towards him. She played with his hair, and he played with hers. He kissed her cheek, and she kissed his. At last their lips met, and it was a long, long time before they drew back to gaze at one another.

After a lot more kisses, long embraces, holding of hands and stroking of hair and faces, she spoke. 'My father will be expecting me. He'll be worried if I don't get back soon. I don't want him to come looking and find me like this, lying on a bank and kissing a big handsome stranger.'

'Go on then,' he said reluctantly. 'But tell me your name.'

'Only if you tell me yours.' She smiled and stroked his chest.

'Of course I will, but you tell me yours first.'

'Consuela.'

'Of course it is. What else could someone as wonderful as you be called? You are my beautiful Consuela.' He tried to kiss her, but she pushed him away.

'Not until you tell me yours.'

'My name is Perico. I live over there, in the house by the lake.' He pointed.

She had worked on the farm since the age of five, and was strong. The punch that landed on his mouth hurt, and knocked his head backwards. 'Why did I think you were so perfect and wonderful, and that you loved me?' Her fierce voice shocked Perico. Another punch landed on his eye and drew blood. His head rang as if a pumpkin had hit it. She cursed herself. 'I am so stupid.'

He grabbed her wrist. 'What are you doing?' he cried. She was too quick for him and wrestled free, raining blows all over his head and chest.

Dazed, he grabbed her arms again and implored, 'Just tell me why you're doing this. Tell me.'

'Do you think I'm stupid? Everyone knows you're going to marry a rich girl from one of the big houses. Everyone. You're treating me worse than you would a pet worm. You have no feelings for me, you're just a filthy dirty ram.' Perico, his father's eldest son, was well known and highly regarded. Consuela's old father had often joked about them marrying, but they knew he would never marry a girl from a little farm. Again she wrestled free, and began landing more punches on him. 'Oh, I've heard all about you,' she said, beating him in the belly as he tried to push her away. 'About how handsome you are and how charming. And you are handsome and you are charming, but really you are a very unpleasant man. Goodbye forever.'

Consuela's world was in tatters. Since she had been a little girl she had dreamed of her first kiss, and how perfect it would be. This sordid fumble had broken her heart. What had seemed so wonderful had become little more than one of the dreadful stories the other girls told her on market day.

She had never wanted to be like them but now, it seemed, she was no different at all.

She walked back to her mule as Perico lay doubled up, winded. She untied it and set off home, but Perico struggled to his feet, caught up with her and gasped, 'Let me explain.'

'Tell lies, you mean.' Her face was red, her lips were pouting and her chest was heaving in anger.

'No. Listen.' Again he struggled for breath. 'I love you and I want to marry you.'

'You don't mean that.'

'I do. Listen. It's true that I was going to marry one of those rich girls, but I can never love them now. Not now I've met you. I thought I could have loved one of them, but now I realise I had no idea what love was until I saw you driving your mule through the woods.'

'Oh, and I'm sure you'll promise to love me too, until you stumble across another little thing, ripe for kissing as she drives her mule through the woods. I'm not stupid.'

'I know you're not stupid. That's partly why I love you. I love everything about you. Listen. Tomorrow at eight, come with your father to my family's house. I'll introduce you to my parents, you'll see that I'm sincere and you'll be able to think about marrying me.'

She thought. After all, she had never seen anyone quite as handsome as him before, and he had seemed to be so gentle and strong. Maybe he really did love her. 'All right then. I'll see you tomorrow.'

'And will you marry me?'

'If you're genuine, then of course I'll marry you. If you're not genuine, then . . . ' She pummelled her right fist into her left palm.

He smiled and his lips flew towards her face. She offered only a cold cheek, and strode towards her father's cottage.

'Tomorrow,' he cried, so happy he could barely feel the wounds on his face. 'Tomorrow, my beautiful Consuela.'

The ladybird flew from her hair and up into the warm air.

Perico told his family about beautiful Consuela.

'Mother, father, her hair is so long, and her face, oh, I have never seen such a perfect face, not even in a painting or the wildest corner of my imagination. Her eyes are so big and . . .'

'No,' roared his father. 'You're not marrying her.'

'But how can I marry Inez or Juanita when my heart is tied, no, chained to Consuela's pretty face?'

'You're not marrying a random doe-eyed peasant girl you just happened to have met in the woods. Tomorrow we'll pick your bride and set a date for the wedding.'

'Of course we must set a date for the wedding, but my wedding to Consuela, not to anyone else.'

'You stupid boy,' interjected his mother. 'Do you really

expect us to open our hearts to a grubby little milk-maid? We haven't come this far to have you spoil everything by marrying some farm girl.'

Perico couldn't help but feel guilty, but he was resolute. 'I can't do it. I'll never be able to forget her.'

'You will. And anyway, who did that to you?' she asked, pointing at the livid blotches and crusts of dried blood on his face.

Perico looked into the air, smiled and said, 'Consuela.' For a moment the sound of her name brushed all his cares aside and ignited a firework display in his heart. 'My beautiful Consuela.'

Perico's parents finally agreed to meet Consuela. 'Very well. If it keeps you quiet, but don't for a moment expect us to change our minds about this ridiculous situation.' His mother even began to look forward to it, and started to work out ways of greeting this delightful little peasant.

Perico spent most of the day in the grounds dreaming of Consuela, of the touch of her fingers and the beauty of her eyebrows. He prayed that she hadn't been eaten by a wolf or met anyone else since the day before. He gazed at his reflection in the lake, loving all the scratches and bruises, and wishing they would last forever.

The agreed time arrived, and Perico's mother was consumed with excitement at the thought of meeting her prospective daughter-in-law. She had decided not to have her whipped and basted with hot fat on this occasion, but in the unlikely event of her ever attempting to contact Perico again, the dirt-encrusted harlot would wish she hadn't.

The gong called the family to the table.

'Where is your pretty fiancée, Perico?' asked his mother as the first course arrived.

'I don't know. She's on her way.' There was not a great deal of conversation.

'You know, I can't tell you how much I'm looking forward to meeting her.' It was obvious to Perico that his mother was planning something terrible, and he worried about what she would say or do to his future wife. Part of him didn't care. Whatever happened he would be with Consuela, even if it meant leaving everything behind him and spending the rest of his life on the farm.

'I do hope she hasn't decided that it just isn't worth the journey.'

Perico was despondent. Before long he decided that his mother was right; Consuela was not going to turn up, and the romance was over. He wished the world would end, and could do nothing but push his food around his plate until the door opened, a servant walked in and his mother flushed with excitement, drank the last of her wine and rose to her feet.

'Señorita Consuela and her father,' announced the servant,

with an unusual tremor in his voice. Consuela's white-bearded father entered the room, followed by his daughter.

In a flash, Perico's mother was within inches of the girl. 'Listen you . . .' she shrieked, stopping still. She looked with contempt at Consuela. 'Listen you . . .' At the ragged dress of this scheming peasant who had come to move into the enormous house they had finally built after so many years of hardship and struggle. 'Listen you . . .' At the orchids in her hair, at her big, brown eyes that darted around the room taking in all the new faces, the majesty of the gallery of stuffed cadavers, and the trophies gleaned from countless voyages to the New World. 'Listen you . . .' At the nervous look on her unblemished face. 'Listen you . . .' she spat, somehow unable to begin the abuse she had rehearsed so thoroughly. Consuela started to shake, and held her father's arm. Perico's mother moved towards her, stopping only when her face was an inch away from the trembling girl's. 'Listen you . . .'

She could shout no more at this petrified angel.

She looked at Perico, standing ashen by the dinner table, then back at the girl who had so comprehensively captured her heart. Her voice softened. 'Listen, you mustn't worry about being late. You had so far to come. More wine,' she called to a servant. Consuela and her father took their places at the table, Consuela beside Perico, where she could rub her leg against his without anyone seeing.

*

Consuela's father grew weary after all the food and wine, and the time came for them to begin the long journey back to their cottage. The family gathered around its new member. They bade farewell to the pretty girl whom Perico had, so rightly, chosen to marry. His mother showered her with kisses, hugged her, stroked her hair and face, and implored the poor motherless child to call her mamá.

The fathers agreed on a date for the wedding: three weeks thence, on Consuela's sixteenth birthday.

It was not long before everyone had heard that Perico had become engaged to a girl he had met in the woods. From the windows of mansions and castles came the sound of young hearts breaking.

The wedding was wonderful. In her simple white dress, Consuela looked perfect as she stood beside her husband at the altar.

Consuela had always dreamed of wearing beautiful dresses and jewels, and loved all the clothes and trinkets her new mamá had made for her. At balls and banquets she shone like a star as she hung on to her husband's arm. Even so, every afternoon, after her dancing and harp lessons, she would slip into her old brown dress and visit her father and the mule on the farm they had been given just beyond the grounds of the house. Even though Perico glowed with pride whenever they were out in public in their finery, he always thought she looked most beautiful of all when she became once again the girl he had seen that day in the woods. He felt her jewels and elaborate clothes to be a little gaudy and obtrusive next to her natural beauty, and if she hadn't loved wearing them so much he would have told her not to bother. Whenever he could he went with her to the farm, and they spent endless afternoons collecting eggs, picking little green apples from the trees and sitting by the stream, dangling their feet in the water and kissing. It seemed nothing could ever shatter the harmony of their lives.

On their return to the house Consuela would bathe, then practise on the harp they had in their room. All through her years on the farm she had hummed tunes to herself and the animals, and always had music flying through her mind. Now, with her harp lessons and plenty of practice, she was able to make these tunes real. Every evening before they went down to dinner she sat naked at the instrument, gently plucking its strings as her husband sat behind her, brushing her wet hair, watching her back gently ripple as she played, and loving every note of the music. Often, after they had made love she would play a mournful tune in D-minor as Perico listened and watched.

During these perfect days, this music was the only sad thing in their lives.

*

Perico received a letter from Juanita. She had managed to convince herself that she was going to be his chosen bride, and told him that should anything terrible ever happen to Consuela, she would always be there for him.

She was right. Had he not stumbled across his beloved Consuela in the woods, Perico would certainly have married her.

'Who's the letter from?' asked Consuela, as Perico opened and read it on the other side of the room.

'No one. It's just some boring business.'

'So now I know.' She looked away. 'You would rather read boring letters than kiss your wife. It's such a shame it had to end this way.' She took her wedding ring from her finger and threw it hard at Perico's forehead, leaving a small red mark. Her bottom lip stuck out as she enjoyed every moment of this conflict.

Quite used to these delicious tantrums, Perico folded the letter and put it to one side. He picked up the ring from the floor and went over to Consuela, who was sprawled petulantly across the bed. After a long struggle he pushed the ring back on her finger and slowly began to kiss every inch of her soft skin, starting with the soles of her feet.

But Perico had to go away. One day he would take over his father's business, and to do such a thing required the kind of experience that could not be acquired through kissing alone.

He set to sea as part of a routine expedition to collect spices, plants, animals, fabrics and precious ornaments from the New World. He looked back at the shore until Consuela became a barely perceptible, yet indescribably beautiful, black speck. He knew she would be there watching until the horizon swallowed the masts of the ship. Then she would return home and count the days until his return.

Every moment was purgatory. Perico could not find joy in anything.

He was taken to a mountain range.

'Aren't they beautiful?' asked someone from the expedition, looking in awe at the snow-capped peaks that were so much more gigantic and terrifying than anything he had ever seen at home.

'No. No, they're not,' replied Perico. The mountains had reminded him of the perfect breasts of his young bride, yet they did not possess anything even approaching the same magnificence.

Every night he declined invitations to join the revels of the other young men away from home. Instead he remained on his own, imagining Consuela was with him in his cabin or his tent, running her fingers through his hair and humming a pretty tune she had thought up while working on the farm.

Every day was agony for Consuela too. She wrote a hundred tunes for him and planned a thousand ways of welcoming him home. She practised her reading and writing, and composed long poems about her sadness and her love for him. Whether she slept on the farm or at the house, she wept every night and stroked the empty space beside her.

Before long it became apparent that she would have a very special gift for him on his return.

Juanita heard of his voyage, and was haunted by visions of his ship coming to grief on a vicious foreign rock. Every night she woke trembling, cold and damp with sweat. She had almost convinced herself that she would never see her Perico again, that his body had been dragged below the waves, and that even his final, desperate cry of 'Juanita' could not save him.

Before the return voyage he visited the remains of the principal city of a long-fragmented civilisation.

'Isn't it incredible?' asked a man of about Perico's age, who was standing next to him and trying to imagine it as it had been all those centuries ago, when these abandoned structures had been the centre of a vibrant culture.

'No,' replied Perico, comparing the view to his memory of the small of his wife's back. It was so smooth and perfect. 'No, not really.'

The ship was packed with a cargo of silks, spices,

precious metals, jewels, trinkets and ornaments, including many things that had never been seen on their side of the world. Perico's single contribution was a small cluster of flowering plants. They had been the only thing that had captured his attention for the whole expedition, and he worried that they would wither and die before they reached home. The plant produced fantastic flowers, but it was not the striking red and blue of their petals that had drawn him to them; instead it was their smell. They smelled pure, sweet and strangely like his wife as she lay in his arms after they had made love. They were turning brown and falling off, but he had been assured that every year they would return to bloom with their scent every bit as evocative. He looked forward to growing them everywhere; in the gardens of the house, in every room, and all over the nearby villages. He would nurture and breed them, and make a gift of one to every person he met and liked. He thought of a name for this plant. He called it Beautiful Consuela.

He returned to find Consuela not as he had left her, but blooming in expectation of their first child. That same evening she gave birth to a lovely, crumpled baby girl. Unable to be apart from her in this time of joyful agony, Perico held her hand and mopped her brow as the child appeared. He named her after her mother. Little Consuela.

Consuela's figure snapped straight back into its original

shape. Within two days she was back on the farm and, were it not for the tiny bundle strapped to her back, no one would have known she had so recently become a mother as she darted from field to field, helping her father in any way she could.

Juanita heard of the birth and wrote another letter. She told Perico that she was much prettier than he would remember her, and assured him that should the unthinkable ever happen to Consuela, she would love the child as her own.

As if to make room for Little Consuela, the old mule dropped dead. Consuela was inconsolable for days. She wept as she bade farewell to her lifelong friend. As he was lowered into his deep grave on the farm, she was comforted by the adoring arms of her husband and father. They planted a bed of Beautiful Consuela where he lay.

Perico was sad about the mule too, but his grief was far outweighed by the pleasure he gleaned from being there for his wife; hugging her, kissing and stroking her face, telling her that the mule had enjoyed a long and happy life, and that he was sure everything was going to be fine in the end. And, for a while, everything returned to normal.

Their fifth wedding anniversary was also Consuela's twenty-first birthday. Perico, with more than a little help from the cooks, prepared a meal of Consuela's favourite dishes: olives, salmon straight from the stream, lamb from the farm and all the fresh vegetables she loved. Mamá and the nurse doted on Little Consuela for the night, dandling her on their knees and singing songs about gypsies, tramps and thieves that they remembered from their own childhoods. The couple were able to shut themselves away from everyone else and spend the evening eating, talking and looking at each other.

Consuela enjoyed every mouthful, and they swilled the food down with twenty-one-year-old red wine. The meal was rounded off with a selection of cheeses. They were arranged in pieces on a board, and each was carved in the shape of a letter. Together they spelled 'Happy Birthday Beautiful Consuela'. She laughed when she saw it, and ate the chunk that was the n of her name. He ate the C.

'Have some more,' said Perico.

'No, I couldn't.'

'Go on, have another bit.'

'No, I'll burst if I eat any more. Really.'

'Well, all right then. I suppose I'd better not feed you up any more. After all, we don't want you getting any fatter, do we?' He went to get another bottle of wine, and as he passed her he pinched her cheek and wobbled it.

Since the death of the mule, Consuela had put on about seven pounds.

Triste

Perico realised that he should not have mentioned Consuela's extra weight. Her wedding ring was on the table and, for the first time since their fight in the woods, her anger was real.

'I thought you loved me.' Her eyes were fixed on her empty plate.

'Of course I love you.'

'No you don't.'

'I'm sorry, Consuela.'

'What for?'

'For saying you're fat.'

'You mean you're sorry for telling the truth.'

'You're not fat.'

'I am fat. Why else would you wobble my cheek? My big, fat cheek.'

'Consuela, you're the most beautiful person I've ever seen. You know that.'

'Only because you keep telling me. How am I supposed to know you mean it? And anyway, I'm putting on weight so I won't be so beautiful for much longer will I?'

'You're hardly a big fat pig, are you?'

'But what if I was? What if I was a big fat pig? Would you still love me?'

Perico tried a joke to clear the air. 'Of course I wouldn't. I'm not going to be married to a barrel of grease.'

173

Consuela did not smile. 'You shouldn't love me for my weight. I haven't changed, you know. I'm still the same person you married. You should love me for what I am, not how much I weigh.'

'Of course I love you for what you are, Consuela.' There was an awful silence.

'I'll leave if you don't want me any more,' she mumbled. 'I won't cause a fuss, I'll go quietly. I never expected this to last anyway. Not really. It was always too perfect to be real. You can find a slim wife and I'll go back to my father. At least he still loves me.'

Perico walked over to his wife, pulled her towards him, kissed her cheek and ran his fingers through her wonderful long brown curls.

'And I still love you too. Of course I love you, and I always will.' He really believed this. He could not imagine a world in which he was not hopelessly in love with her. 'Consuela, I love you.'

'Do you mean it?' She was pouting beautifully.

'Yes. I do.'

At last she looked at him and saw the love in his eyes. She tried not to, but she smiled. She didn't struggle as Perico put the ring back on her finger.

Consuela could not get the incident out of her mind. She threw herself into her work on the farm, and was often to be found in the kitchen helping the cooks with the family meal. Even so, Perico's words that night rang constantly in her ears, and her cheek burned as she recalled the time he had wobbled her face. It seemed to be an order to lose weight, to be perfect for him. He loved what he saw and nothing else. He was always telling her how pretty she was, as if nothing else was important to him. Often she found herself shaking and had to rush off to be alone for a few moments as she told herself that he did love her and there was nothing to be frightened about.

She found comfort in the cheese produced by the small dairy herd her father had bought, and in morsels from the kitchen. The songs she played on her harp became more desolate than ever as she struggled to find a way of knowing for certain that he loved her.

One night, as she lay in her husband's arms with her eyes closed, smelling as sweet as a bed of Beautiful Consuela, she felt a kiss brush her forehead, then a finger trace a line down her nose, across her lips and onto her chin, where it remained. 'You are so beautiful, Consuela,' said her husband. Without her eyes opening, tears rolled down her cheeks.

Thinking them to be the tears of contentment she had so often shed, Perico drifted into an untroubled sleep.

Consuela could not sleep at all. Perico's words had served to confirm her fears. He didn't love her. Not really. All he wanted was her beauty. She clung to her husband and tried to tell herself that she was wrong, but it didn't work. He loved her for the softness of her skin, for the way her big brown eyes were set in her pretty face, for her sweet smell, for the curls that tumbled down her back, and for her gentle, musical voice. He didn't love her for what she was.

Her grief was compounded by the shocking thought that maybe poor Perico didn't even know that the feelings he had mistaken for total, endless love were really no more than the animal stirrings of his passion. She wondered if she could ever make him see what she was really like inside, and love her for it.

In her misery she found solace in stealthy mouthfuls of meat. Her dresses began to pinch.

Everyone noticed the change in Consuela's size, but nobody mentioned it to her. Whispers swept the area that the big house by the lake would soon be blessed with the wailing of another tiny pair of lungs, but before long it became apparent that this would not be so.

Perico enjoyed his wife's new weight because it gave him even more of her to love. It was evenly spread across her body, and she wore it well. Nuzzling his way into each new roll of fat became a glorious voyage of discovery.

More and more of her clothes became unwearable and one night, as he was sitting behind her at the harp, brushing her lustrous hair, kissing her shoulders and loving the sad music, he noticed a line of blotches around her waist where her clothing had rubbed her skin raw. He said nothing. Still, he marvelled at the way she looked. But Consuela knew that every time he praised her beauty he was really telling her, even if he didn't know it, that he didn't love her and never had done. Despite this, she couldn't bring herself to leave him. Even if he didn't love her, she still loved him with all her heart, and she desperately tried to work out ways of making him love her. The real her, not the imaginary person the poor boy had unknowingly constructed around the framework of her pretty appearance.

She ran out of clothes, and went to see a woman in the village who, in exchange for a bundle of eggs and fruit, made her a new dress. She was wearing it when Perico arrived home from a visit to a nearby trader's house.

'What are you wearing?' he asked.

'My new dress.'

'Oh.' He didn't know what to say. It looked as if she had become entangled in a sack. The dress was nothing more than a swathe of coarse, grey-brown cloth with a hole for her head and one for each of her arms. It fell to the ground like a tent. He kissed her, just as he had every time he had ever returned from being away from her. However, he did not comment on how incredible she looked, as he had done every time she had previously appeared in a new outfit.

'How was your day?'

'Fine. Yours?' Usually they spent ages dissecting every moment they had spent apart.

'Busy. I worked on the farm. Went to get this dress made. This and that.'

'Ah.' He kissed her again and pulled her towards him. Used to feeling his wife's body through silk or the soft, thin material of her farm dress, this sackcloth grated against his hand. He stroked her exposed forearm but his face could not conceal the disappointment he felt at this new addition to her wardrobe. Usually the first thing he did when she showed him a new dress was to find a way of slipping his hand inside and touching her body. This dress was far too unwieldy to allow it.

'Don't you like it?' she asked.

'I didn't say that.'

'I know you didn't, but I can tell.'

Perico kissed her cheek and smiled. 'It's not very flattering, Consuela.'

'Why should it be?'

'Well, it's just I'm used to you wearing pretty clothes.'

'But they're only clothes. They're not me. All they do is cover me up.'

'I know, but this just isn't very nice, is it?'

'Why should it be? What difference does it make to you?'

'Listen. Tomorrow mamá will take you to the dressmaker

and buy you beautiful gowns just like before, and any time you want a new dress you can have one made. Don't worry about saving money.'

'Why should I get new clothes made? What's the point? You only need them to keep you from being naked. They're so unimportant.'

'But Consuela, this is horrible. You're so beautiful, but it makes you look like a bag of turnips.'

'And you love me less because of it.' She was unable to resist being so direct.

'Of course I don't love you less.'

'Then why are you demanding that I wear different clothes?'

'I'm not demanding anything, I'm just saying . . .'

'Just saying that you don't love me and never have done. All you worry about is me looking pretty on your arm. If you loved me, you would love me for what I am, not for the clothes I wear. You wouldn't even notice what I was wearing. I'm still the same person you married, you know. How could something as unimportant as clothes make a difference?' Consuela wept, looking occasionally at the confused and wonderful face of the man she adored.

Perico couldn't stand his wife questioning the depth of his love, and desperately tried to make sense of all this. He had always found her most beautiful of all in her simple brown dress, so why should she not wear this shapeless sackcloth?

He looked at her hair, which still shone like the night sky, at her crying brown eyes, her wonderful lips that quivered in time with every sob. His love pierced the transient fabric, and rested warmly on the wife beyond. She was right. Her new dress just didn't matter.

'I love you, Consuela.' He peppered her cheeks, forehead, nose and double-chin with kisses until she responded, yielding at last to his love-making. 'I love you no matter what you wear.'

'Really?'

'Really. I'm sorry I've been so horrible, Consuela.'

That night, as the dress lay in a heap beside the bed, she was prepared to believe him. Perico drifted off to sleep as his wife plucked a tune from her harp, humming gentle harmonies as she played.

The short walk to the farm became more and more difficult, and when she got there she couldn't work nearly as hard as she had done. Instead of rushing from field to field, she restricted her chores to the house. She dusted, washed and cooked for her father, helping herself to any scraps she fancied as Little Consuela toddled happily in the yard.

One evening Perico came home to find she had just returned from the farm and was slumped in a heap on the bed, exhausted and sweating. Rings of moisture from her armpits and back darkened the heavy cloth of her dress, and streams tumbled down her face.

He kissed her shining forehead. 'You look like you've had a hard day.'

'Oh, just normal really.'

He held her hand and played with her fingers as she caught her breath.

'You should have a bath. Freshen up.'

'Maybe later.'

The bath didn't happen. She knew that if he really loved her then her size, her clothes and her sweat marks would mean nothing to him. Would a loving eye see them as faults? Would it see them at all? It should only see the perfection within. The moisture evaporated, leaving dry crusts on her dress. When bedtime came and they made love, Perico enjoyed the primal smell of sweat coming from his wife, and as he licked her salty flesh he tasted ambrosia and imagined he had just found her living wild in a cave.

When, three days later, she still hadn't washed, the sweat grew stale and the fantasy began to pall. 'Why don't you have a quick bath, Consuela?'

'Why?'

He braced himself. 'You're starting to get a bit smelly, that's all. Just a bit.'

'I asked why.'

'And I told you why.'

'Because I don't smell the way you think I should?'

'Well, you could just do with a dip, that's all. We both could. It's hot.'

'I'll only start sweating again as soon as I get out. There's no point.'

'But Consuela, you stink.'

She looked out of the window. 'You don't love me, do you?' she mumbled.

'Of course I love you.'

'If you loved me you wouldn't worry about what I smell like. You should love me for what I am, for what's inside, not because I happen to smell as sweet as a flower. I'm still the same person you married. I haven't changed just because I smell different.'

'I know, Consuela, and of course I love you for what's inside. I just can't see why you won't have a bath.' The rings of sweat had left permanent tide-marks on her sackcloth.

'I've told you. If you loved me for what I am you wouldn't even notice what I smelled like.' No, he didn't love her, and never had done. She reached for her wedding ring, to quietly give it back to him and leave without any fuss. It was wedged on to her finger. She became angrier the harder she tried to pull it off.

Perico couldn't bear to see her like this. He looked at her beautiful curls, her big brown eyes and her smooth skin. He ignored the stained, ugly dress, and tried to imagine that the stench was nothing more than an unpleasant farm odour wafted into the room by an unlucky breeze. He kissed her reddened ring-finger, and told her that he loved her.

She lay down as he made love to her, prepared for that moment to believe him. He frantically tried to work out ways of making her see that he really loved her and always would, no matter what.

Consuela loved sweet food. Because she no longer took care of her teeth, it wasn't long before they turned yellow, then brown, and started to decay.

'If you loved me you'd kiss me,' she would say to Perico.

'Come here,' he would say, before inhaling a lungful of relatively clean air, holding it in and drawing his wife towards him for a short, breathless kiss. Sometimes he wasn't able to withdraw from her clutches before having to take another breath, and the hot, horrible stench from her mouth and sweating body would make him retch.

'See. You don't love me, do you?'

He would look at her lovely long brown hair and remember the time he had first seen her. 'I do love you, Consuela. Please believe me.'

She stopped doing whatever it was she had done to keep her body smooth. Her legs, arms and yellow-brown armpits became covered in a carpet of dark hairs.

She had grown to more than three times her original weight.

Consuela ventured out from her room less and less. On her rare trips to the market, people pitied this poor woman in her stained brown sack, with her shiny face which, through neglect, had become pockmarked and rough, and her lips which were distorted into an ever-changing shapelessness by her absence of teeth. When she spoke her voice was muffled by the layers of fat around her throat and mouth, and her tongue slipped unchecked in and out, sending little balls of spit flying for yards. The few remaining black stumps jutting from her gums inspired pity and revulsion as she lumbered her way through the streets. Sometimes children would shout cruel comments and run away, knowing there was no way this slow-moving creature would catch them. They found it hard to believe that not so long ago she had been so startlingly beautiful.

She took her huge meals in her room, and it was her father who now visited her. Little Consuela loved her mother but hated her smell, so she spent most of her time with mamá and her nurse, drawing pictures of her favourite animals and playing her piccolo. Perico always made sure he spent a lot of time with his daughter every day. He loved her. With her pretty, happy ways she reminded him of the way his wife used to be.

*

Perico and Consuela spent their evenings lying on the bed; she emitting incessant wheezes and occasional involuntary squelching noises from deep inside, and wishing her husband loved her; he trying his best to disregard the revolting smells coming from his beloved wife. Whenever he could bear to be close to her, he stroked and kissed her still beautiful hair, the only remaining part of the Consuela he married. He told her that he loved her, and prayed that he meant it. The way his heart pounded when he said it told him that he did.

They made love every night. For a few minutes she became once again the girl beside him at the altar, the one he had dreamed of and longed for when he had been away. When it was over, the stench returned and he looked at her hair, telling her just how beautiful it was and how much he loved her. His beautiful Consuela.

One evening he asked her why she didn't play the harp any more.

She held up her fingers. 'I can't. The strings are too close together.'

She had become disgusting, and if he had not loved her so completely he would have left long before. He was desperate to help her, and knew he had to say something, so one evening he did.

'You're not looking well.'

'What do you mean? I feel fine.'

'I mean you've put on too much weight and you . . .' He paused. 'You should be more careful with your washing. Washing yourself, I mean. Your teeth are horrible and you stink.' It hurt him to be so direct.

Consuela burst into tears. No, he did not love her. He loved the woman he had created in his mind, not her. Her rage spilled out. 'You don't love me.' She drummed her fists on his chest. 'You don't love me and you never did.'

Her words cut into his heart. He loved her more than he could ever articulate, so he just held her wrists until she calmed down. He took her in his arms as her sobs subsided.

'You don't love me,' she whimpered.

'You have no idea how much I love you.' He stroked and kissed her hair. 'No idea at all.'

'You think I'm ugly, you think I smell, you think I'm fat. So you don't love me.' She knew that she was all these things, that she had let herself become this way, but she also knew that they were of negligible importance in a real, loving marriage. Beauty should cease to exist.

'Listen,' he said, stroking her hair. 'I love you just as much as the day we married.' He buried his face in her curls, and prayed that he was telling the truth. The warmth he felt inside told him that he was.

With his father growing older and becoming increasingly disinclined to travel, Perico spent more time visiting business partners and clients. One such merchant was the father of Juanita, the pretty girl he had so nearly married.

They spent an uncomfortable morning discussing business matters. The old man had clearly not forgotten the way Perico had rejected his daughter. Her broken heart had not healed, and she had refused to marry anyone else. She had not been told of his visit, but in the afternoon as he walked around the grounds of their house, she saw him from her window and rushed down to meet him.

'Perico,' she cried, overjoyed.

She seemed so different. Her straight black hair fell to her waist, her tight dress hugged her slender shape and exposed a glimpse of her majestic bosom. He had always thought her very pretty, but she was so much more beautiful than he remembered.

They spent the afternoon together, walking and talking. Her maid, knowing every detail of Juanita's love for him, maintained a discreet distance, and the conversation flowed like Consuela's hair. The pretty smile never left Juanita's face. She took his arm and gazed at him, making no attempt to conceal her passion.

'How is Little Consuela?'

'Oh, she's wonderful. I should have brought her with me.'

'And Consuela?' Everyone knew about Consuela's appearance.

'She's wonderful too.' He couldn't help but look upset at

the thought of his poor wife's condition, and Juanita gently held his hand, stroking his palm with her fingertips. 'Yes, she's wonderful, Juanita,' he said, sadly. 'I'm so in love with her.' He pictured her brown curls, splayed across the pillow, and prayed that the desire he felt was born of the warmth of his love for her.

In the pear orchard she put her arms around his neck and kissed him.

'No, Juanita. Please,' he said, gently pushing her away. 'You mustn't do this.'

Her hand slipped inside his shirt, where it stayed, gently stroking his body. 'I knew I would see you again one day, Perico.'

He pulled the beautiful woman's hand away and backed off. 'I'm sorry, Juanita. I mustn't. I'm married to Consuela. I love her, Juanita. I'm sorry. I just don't want to do this with you.'

Again she flew at him, pushing her breasts into his body and kissing his closed lips. 'I love you, Perico. I love you. Everyone knows Consuela's fat and ugly. They laugh at her. Make love to me. I'll be your mistress if I can't be your wife.' Again she slipped her hand under his shirt. 'Any time you want me, I'll be here for you. I've saved myself for you. You know that, don't you? Kiss me, Perico.' He pushed her away.

He ran to his horse, pursued by Juanita and her maid, who had been watching from behind a tree and wondering what to do. He was overcome with desire. He galloped away, his loins burning, in the direction of the wife whom, he kept telling himself, he loved more than anything else on earth. 'Consuela, Consuela, Consuela,' he whispered in time with the horse's hoofs. He told himself that he would never want Juanita, and that the longing he felt was to stroke and kiss those long brown curls that had somehow managed to retain their beauty as the rest of his wife had disintegrated.

Consuela hated her hair. He spent so much time playing with it, kissing it and telling her how beautiful it was. It had nothing to do with what she was inside.

As Perico was galloping back to her, she summoned a maid and told her to get rid of all this horrible hair. Unable to bear the smell for longer than a couple of minutes, the maid made a mess of the cut, but it complied with Consuela's instructions.

'Short. Very short.'

Her curls lay in a heap on the floor.

Perico called from outside the room. 'Consuela, I'm home.' His pulse raced. He burst in and saw her standing naked, her beautiful shining hair in a pile by her feet and her head covered by uneven clumps of stubble.

'Consuela, no.' He raced to the hair, picked up a handful and hysterically put it back on her head as if it would stay there and everything would return to normal. Every time he put a clump on her head it slipped straight back on to the floor, and before long he was so blinded by his tears that he couldn't continue.

He stood a few feet away from his wife, who had more than quadrupled in size since their wedding day. He dried his eyes and looked at the huge purple-veined breasts that rested on top of her enormous hanging gut, at the way her face was twisted out of shape by her despair and absence of teeth, and was pitted and grey from its lack of exposure to sunlight and water. Her skin was rough, and stretched into horrific shapes. It was covered by a salty, slimy, and in some places fishy layer of sweat, grime and stale sex. And her hair, her beautiful hair, had gone. Ugly sobs and squelches came from her mouth. Every time she breathed, globules of saliva dripped down her chin or sprayed on to her belly. Her stench filled his nose and mouth, and seemed to cling to him inside and out; odours so nauseating that he had never encountered them elsewhere. He felt them in the pit of his stomach, and was sure he could even see them, a dull yellow hovering around her. He looked at her legs, at the rolls of fat hanging over her knees, and was it . . . ? Was it . . . ? His eyes took a while to focus through the tears. Yes it was. The tiniest rivulet of diarrhoeal faeces snaked its way down the hairy moonscape of her inner thigh before becoming lost in a fold of skin, and forming, or maybe joining, an underflesh reservoir.

She looked at the floor with a terrible, dead expression, and mumbled, 'You don't love me. Do you?' She couldn't struggle any more. This was the end.

His wife offended every one of his senses. Every single one. But he loved her more than anything in the world, and this love seared through the sight he saw and the way she stank. Her wheezing voice jarred his nerves, but so what? The roughness of her skin meant nothing to him, and neither did its slimy coating. His love battered its way through all this to what was inside. To what she was. His wife, whom he adored.

He threw his arms around her, and kissed her as she had never been kissed, running his fingers across her uneven crop of hair, and slipping his arms up to the elbow in damp folds of fat. For hours they stood together, lost in each other's love. When, finally, time came to stop, he drew back just far enough to look straight into her puffy red eyes.

'I love you, Consuela.' His words rang out with the purity of a church bell on Christmas morning. For the first time in his life he knew he had really meant it, that he did love her, and for the first time in her life Consuela felt loved; loved for what she was. They stood in each other's arms knowing, at last, that they had found true love.